"Helena, are you trying to avoid me?"

Marcos fixed his eyes on her face. "Have I offended you in some way?"

"N-no, of course not. How could you?"

"Then prove it by staying with me, hmm?" He looked down at her. "I don't want you to be nervous about meeting my grandfather. He is not a monster."

"Just a tyrant," she replied.

"A tyrant, maybe," he agreed, "but a loving tyrant, as you will see." As Marcos would be some day, Helena knew with a sudden certainty.

"Why have you never married, Marcos?" She was surprised by her own temerity in asking such a question.

"I have been waiting for my bride to grow up."

ANNABEL MURRAY has pursued many hobbies. She helped found an arts group in Liverpool, England, where she lives with her husband and two daughters. She loves drama; she appeared in many stage productions and went on to write an award-winning historical play. She uses all her experiences—holidays being no exception—to flesh out her characters' backgrounds and create believable settings for her romance novels.

Books by Annabel Murray

HARLEQUIN PRESENTS

933—LAND OF THUNDER
972—FANTASY WOMAN
1029—NO STRINGS ATTACHED
1076—GIFT BEYOND PRICE
1148—A PROMISE KEPT
1188—A QUESTION OF LOVE
1228—DON'T ASK WHY

HARLEQUIN ROMANCE

2549—ROOTS OF HEAVEN
2558—KEEGAN'S KINGDOM
2596—THE CHRYSANTHEMUM AND THE SWORD
2612—VILLA OF VENGEANCE
2625—DEAR GREEN ISLE
2717—THE COTSWOLD LION
2782—THE PLUMED SERPENT
2819—WILD FOR TO HOLD
2843—RING OF CLADDAGH
2932—HEART'S TREASURE
2952—COLOUR THE SKY RED

ANNABEL MURRAY

black lion of skiapelos

Harlequin Books

TORONTO • NEW YORK • LONDON
AMSTERDAM • PARIS • SYDNEY • HAMBURG
STOCKHOLM • ATHENS • TOKYO • MILAN

For Tom—as always.

Harlequin Presents first edition April 1990
ISBN 0-373-11259-9

Original hardcover edition published in 1989
by Mills & Boon Limited

CHAPTER ONE

'I WAS really, really happy.' Lena Thomas paced the living-room of her London flat as she voiced her bewildered distress. 'I had a wonderful job, a wonderful family and—I thought—a wonderful man.' Her full lower lip trembled suddenly and her cornflower-blue eyes were enormous pools of misery in the wan oval of her face. 'Petros and I seemed to have so much in common, not just our work but leisure too. We hardly ever rowed. Where did it all go wrong, Sally?' she entreated her friend, who shrugged helplessly.

'I wish I knew. I'm so sorry.' Curled up in one of the comfortable leather armchairs, Sally sighed sympathetically. Lena turning to her for an opinion was an unusual situation. Until today there had been a tinge of envy in Sally's regard for her friend, literally a golden girl on whom the sun had always shone with such determination. 'It's a crying shame you felt you had to hand in your notice. But with your qualifications you shouldn't have any trouble getting another job, and you still have your marvellous parents,' she concluded in an attempt at comfort.

'But for how much longer?' Lena was in a uncharacteristically pessimistic mood. 'They're not getting any younger.'

'I bet old Domenicos isn't very pleased with his precious great-nephew,' Sally hazarded. She thrived on gossip and longed to extract every detail from the situation. 'He won't like losing you. He always says you're the best PA they've ever had.'

Though Lena was small—five feet nothing in stock-inged feet with a waist men yearned to span—she had an astute brain. Her will to succeed and her sparking nervous energy had taken her to a position of trust within the London-based Greek shipping firm of Theodopoulos and Theodopoulos which operated a large fleet out of England.

Lena's tiny proportions, the long, wilful blonde hair and her tremendous sex appeal made it difficult for those who knew no different to visualise her as a high-powered executive. But over the years Sally had seen her in action, firing questions, delivering answers on shipping and oil companies, drawing at least a dozen threads of her em-ployer's business at once into a neat pattern.

For the past five years Lena's working day had been one of propositions, deals and contracts. News of the Greek firm's activities commanded front-page headlines without losing any of the mystery and intrigue with which such famous names conducted their operations.

Domenicos Theodopoulos prided himself on hearing about big business deals before they were completed, new financing techniques and technical advances before they were perfected, political situations before they arose. Single-minded in his dedication to business, he had never married, and his great-nephew, Petros, was his junior partner and natural successor.

Thus Lena's engagement to Petros Theodopoulos had taken her into a gilded world of the parties her gre-garious and hospitable Greek employer loved. The parties were a means to an end, of course. The talk was still of ships, ships, ships, of big coups and even bigger money, of advantageous marriages—which were in effect business mergers. It was a world where art treasures, racehorses and real estate were discussed and collected as avidly as ships. It was a fascinating and enjoyable world. So now that Lena was no longer to marry the younger Theodopoulos she had lost more than her career.

'I suppose you *could* ask Domenicos for your job back,' Sally suggested. 'Since it means so much to you. Tell him you've changed your mind?'

'No.' Lena paused in her pacing and shook her honey-coloured head. 'He's already got my replacement lined up. Besides, I wouldn't want it back, even if Petros wasn't going to be there.' A shudder ran through her slight frame. 'It would be too humiliating. Everyone knowing what happened, pitying me. I've got to get away, right away where nobody knows me. I shall sell this flat, and make a clean break.'

'I'll miss you. Oh, I could kill Petros Theodopoulos for what he's done to you,' Sally said savagely. However much she might have envied her friend in the past, she hated to see her like this, she realised, Lena's bubbly effervescence deflated, her bright, courageous nature defeated.

In their friendship Lena had always been the strong one to whom Sally had turned for help and advice in numerous crises. It was Lena who, three years ago, had obtained Sally her present secretarial position with the Greek shipping firm.

They'd been friends since schooldays. Both came from the same Essex village, Lena the daughter of a well-to-do farmer and Sally, whose father's shop supplied the village with its groceries. Lena's parents had paid for her to attend the prestigious girls' school. Sally had obtained a scholarship, though only by the skin of her teeth, and had thereafter continued to scrape through exams.

Lena had sailed through them and gone on to obtain a first-class honours degree in business studies.

An only child of elderly parents, she was a high achiever in everything she tackled. Yet Lena always pooh-poohed any suggestion that she was brainier than average. 'It isn't qualifications that count,' she often told her friend. 'It's the will to do things, to really want to get to the top.' And now the fruits of her ambition were to be thrown away.

'Damn Petros!' Sally muttered.

'I suppose it's not really his fault.' Despite her distress, Lena struggled to be fair. She ceased her restless movement and slumped into the other armchair, her whole attitude one of dejection. 'I suppose he couldn't help falling in love with someone else. It could have happened to anyone.'

'It didn't happen to *you*, though, did it?' Sally was still indignant. 'And heaven knows you've had enough opportunities. Men swarm around you like bees round a honeypot,' she said with all the feeling of a plainer girl. 'But *you* stuck to Petros.'

'I loved him,' Lena said. She swallowed convulsively, the nearest she'd come to cracking up since her fiancé had broken the appalling news. For the past two days she'd lived in a numb daze, a sense of unreality possessing her. Now, relating the facts to Sally, unreality became real. She fought back the threatening tears. 'I still love him. That's another reason why I have to go away. I couldn't bear to keep bumping into him and Eva.'

'Well, *I* wouldn't go on loving a man who ditched me a week before the wedding,' Sally pronounced.

'I can't *hate* him,' Lena told her. It would have been vastly better, she reflected, to have had the luxury of hatred. 'He didn't do it on purpose. He was genuinely upset when he told me.'

'I bet!' Less charitable than her friend, Sally was still cynical. 'Of course, it wouldn't have anything to do with the fact that Eva's father is a big man in the Texas oil world? You know what these Greeks are like when it comes to making money! However rich they are, they never seem satisfied. Just think, you could have been filthy rich, too. I reckon you ought to sue him for breach of promise.'

'Sally! Surely you don't think that's all that matters to me? I wouldn't have cared a damn if Petros had been some nine-to-five clerk. It's not his money I'm in love with.'

'No, well——' Sally sounded a little ashamed, but knew *she* could not have discounted wealth so easily. She looked around the comfortable flat that she'd so often coveted. 'So Petros just walks away and gets on with his new romance, leaving *you* to sort this lot out?' A sweep of her hand indicated the vast clutter of wedding presents, some still unopened, the wedding dress, still in its polythene wrapper, now slung carelessly across a chair.

Lena shrugged slender shoulders that looked suddenly frail instead of capable.

'Thank goodness that's one thing I *won't* have to do. Dad's farm secretary's going to come up to town and deal with all this. I rang home just before you arrived, and Dad suggested it.'

Sally had come back from holiday only that afternoon, eagerly anticipating being chief bridesmaid to her best friend at what would surely have been the society wedding of the year, only to find a message saying the marriage was off.

'What on earth did your parents say?' she was avid to know.

'They wanted me to go home, of course. Dad was stunned at first, then furious. He said if he'd been twenty years younger he'd have come up to town and punched Petros on the nose. It was the first time——' she made an odd hiccuping sound, half-sob, half-laughter '—that I've been glad I have elderly parents.'

'And shall you go home?'

'No.' It would have been very easy to run away to her parents comfortable old Essex farmhouse; easy to be a child again in the beloved familiar rooms, with their rough-cast natural stone walls. It would have been comforting to pour out her heart to her mother in the peace and quiet of the chintz-upholstered living-room with its vast inglenook fireplace, hung with Mary Thomas's collection of blue and white china. That was the weakling's way out. Lena was determined to overcome this numbing misery by her own efforts.

'What will you do, then?'

'I'm going abroad for a while. I've always enjoyed travel. In time I might even look for work abroad.'

'You're lucky you don't really *need* to work,' Sally couldn't help commenting.

'Oh, yes, I *do*!' Lena was very positive about that. 'Money isn't all you need for happiness. You need self-respect, too. I'd hate to live an idle existence just because my parents could afford to support me. But that's not the only reason. If I can't be happy, then I've got to keep busy, get tired, so tired that I'll turn off, sleep at night instead of thinking about Petros and Eva—together.'

'Old Domenicos must have heaps of contacts abroad,' Sally pointed out. 'Why not ask him if he knows of anything?'

'He's already suggested it,' Lena admitted.

The elderly Greek had been coldly angry with his great-nephew, concerned, sympathetic and immediately helpful to Lena.

'You must know, Helena——' he always insisted on using her full name '—how sorry I am to lose you, both as an employee and a future member of my family. You wish to go abroad, hmm? Unhappiness does not last forever, my child, and then you will come home. But since you wish to travel there is a great service you can do for me if you will, which could keep you out of England for an unspecified period of time.'

'It sounds exactly what I want.'

'I would like you to go to Athens on my behalf. But I should understand, of course, if you wanted nothing further to do with Greece or Greeks.'

Lena brushed this suggestion aside.

'That would be very silly of me. I've received nothing but kindness from *you*.'

'It is not work, you understand, but nevertheless you will be paid.'

Lena listened with interest as Domenicos Theodopoulos explained.

'Living on the outskirts of London there is a Greek woman, the daughter of...' he hesitated then, 'of a very old friend of mine. Against her father's wishes, Irini married an Englishman. Since then, she has never re-visited her home. Now she has to go into hospital for a serious operation.' Domenicos's deeply lined face was grave. 'The prognosis is not good. It is too late perhaps for her to be reconciled with her father, but she wishes her children to visit their Greek relations, in case...' He did not need to go on. 'Irini asked *me* to accompany her son and daughter, but there are reasons...' He spread his hands in a gesture with which Lena was familiar. It meant he did not intend to enlarge on the subject. 'Instead I promised to find a suitable companion. Working for me, you have learned much about Greece and Greek ways.'

'What about Irini's husband?'

'Dead. Killed in an accident just before the birth of the younger child. It is since then that Irini's health has deteriorated.'

Sally saw them off at the airport.

'You will keep in touch?'

'I'll write,' Lena promised.

'Remember, I'll want to know all about the dishy men you meet. The quickest way to get over a broken romance is to find yourself another one.'

'Love on the rebound? No, thanks,' Lena said drily. 'I think I'll avoid men for a while.'

However many times she travelled, Lena always marvelled at the almost magically swift transit from one country to another. It seemed that the taste of her very British cup of tea had scarcely faded from her palate when she was engulfed by the cosmopolitan atmosphere of a foreign airport.

This flight was no exception, she thought as, only three and a half hours after leaving London, islands and places that she knew only as enchanted names rose out of the sea below—tiers of brown, grey and violet mountains and the huge, towering mass of Parnassus.

As a child, and even into her teens, a romantically inclined Lena had been fascinated by tales of Greek mythology. For a long time she had been promising herself a trip to Greece. Working for a Greek firm had increased her curiosity to see that country, but until now there had been no opportunity. In previous years, as an only child, she had felt duty-bound to accompany her parents on family holidays. Not that it had been an irksome duty. She loved her parents and enjoyed their society, but the Thomases were not fond of overseas travel.

Then, when she'd become engaged to Petros, he'd persuaded her to wait until their honeymoon—'on one of our idyllic islands', he'd promised. That idyll had not transpired.

Many girls in her situation, Lena supposed, might have avoided scenes that should have held such happiness. But she was unlikely to be doing any island-hopping. Athens would be about the limit to this visit. And, as she'd told Domenicos, despite Petros's defection, she felt no bitterness towards his country or his countrymen.

For the most part the journey had been a pleasant one. Irini's children were quiet and well behaved. There was a considerable difference in their ages. Stephen, the younger, was not yet five. To him the journey to meet his Greek relatives was an adventure. To his sister Chryssanti, taller than Lena and nearing her eighteenth birthday, it was more of an ordeal. Unlike her brother, she was not in blissful ignorance of her mother's poor health, and she was finding it hard to control her fears and unhappiness.

'I know Mum's seriously ill,' Chrys, as she preferred to be called, told Lena when Stephen was out of earshot. And, with a little quiver in her voice, 'I think she knows she's going to die.' Despite her own knowledge, Lena felt bound to make an exclamation of protest, but the girl nodded her red-gold head. 'Otherwise why would she be so keen for us to go to Greece to our "rich relations" after all these years? I don't *want* to meet the Mavroleons after the way they treated Mum when she married Dad. I didn't want to be out of England while Mum had her operation. I'd rather have stayed with Nan and Gramps Forster, my father's parents. They're not very well off, but *they* love Stephen and me—*and Mum*. They're not prejudiced against Greeks the way my mother's father was prejudiced against Dad.'

'I don't think it was a question of prejudice,' Lena told her gently. 'It's just that it's the custom in Greece for marriages to be arranged. Mr Theodopoulos told me your mother was to marry a neighbour's son, but she refused and ran away with your father.'

'Good for her,' Chrys retorted. 'I'd just like to see anyone try to make *me* marry someone I didn't fancy. They couldn't do it.'

Lena believed her. There was a lot of Irini Forster in her daughter, even though Chryssanti had inherited her father's bright hair. Lena had spent a few days in Irini's household getting to know the boy and girl with whom she was to be entrusted. She had conceived a deep admiration for the older woman, and not only for her bravery in the face of her illness. Conversant with Greek tradition, Lena knew it must have taken a very special courage to stand out against tradition and her parents' wishes, to leave home for a very different culture and way of life.

As the plane swiftly lost height, the Bay of Athens sparkled with the brilliance of an artist's watercolour, and beyond into the distance, Lena could see a scattering of seemingly endless islands.

Athens airport, and they exchanged the air-
conditioned interior of the aeroplane for the hottest
country in Europe, for sun-baked tarmac and a dazzling
impression of white buildings backed by green hillsides.

They encountered no difficulty at Customs. The
limousine that Domenicos Theodopoulos kept in Athens
was there to meet them. From the airport the road followed the coastline, affording wonderful views of the
sea, blue as flax, with glimpses of the islands of Salamis
and Aegina. In Athens itself Lena craned her neck for
her first view of the Acropolis but, disappointingly, it
was screened from view by tall blocks of offices and
apartment buildings.

One of these buildings was owned by Domenicos
Theodopoulos, and his own penthouse suite was at
Lena's disposal for the duration of her stay. From this
base she was to make contact with the Mavroleon family.

'I take it they don't have a London branch?' she'd
asked.

'No,' he said shortly, and Lena, used to Domenicos's
ways, sensed something underlying the curt negative.

'Isn't that a little... unusual?'

But Domenicos's only answer was a noncommittal
shrug. Whatever his thoughts on the subject, he was obviously not prepared to share them with her. Accustomed during her years of employment to being in full
receipt of the elderly Greek's confidence, Lena was a
little hurt by his reticence. But then, she reminded herself,
by her own choice she was no longer his personal
assistant.

Perhaps Domenicos recognised her chagrin.

'I do not know where my old friend Thalassios can
be found these days,' he had explained, and to her surprise, 'To tell you the truth, the last time we parted it

was not as friends. And since his retirement his company is run by his grandsons, of whom I know little or nothing.'

Lena hadn't liked to ask the cause of the disagreement between Domenicos and Thalassios Mavroleon, and she was a little disconcerted when the elderly Greek added, 'It would be better not to mention my involvement in Irini's affairs. It might be misunderstood.'

'But then how do I explain *my* involvement?' she'd asked.

'You will think of a reason. I have great faith in you, my dear Lena.' Which was flattering, but unhelpful.

Lena slept badly that first night in Athens. Despite all her brave efforts to put her charges' interests before her own, she was still bitterly unhappy. For a while after Petros had ended their relationship there had been the hope that he would contact her, tell her it had all been a dreadful mistake. But gradually that hope had faded and, with its fading, the iron had entered into her soul. She'd left England fiercely determined in future to erect a protective shell about her emotions and to put the young Greek out of her thoughts. But it wasn't easy.

Like Sally, some people might think that it was the loss of her career, the wealthy life-style that marriage to Petros would have provided, that mattered to Lena. But she'd loved him for himself, not the material prospects he offered. And there was the gnawing physical deprivation, too. Though she and Petros had never made love in the full physical sense, his kisses and caresses had aroused her to a need that their marriage would have satisfied. It was a need that could not be lulled to sleep as easily as it had been awoken.

At first light she gave up the struggle for sleep, pulled a négligé around her slender shoulders and wandered out on to the rooftop terrace, a very acceptable substitute for a garden, and gave her thoughts full rein. Oh, Petros!

It was so early that the dust and fumes from traffic had not yet begun to rise. The air was still cool and sweet. A lemon and honey light cast a spell over the surrounding mundane buildings. And—Lena caught her breath—there was the view that had eluded her last night. Rising serenely above its modern neighbours was the Acropolis, its pale classic lines reflecting the dawn in blushing pink. She stood there for a long time allowing the vision to work its ancient magic. When she finally moved, it was with a new energy. Somehow the sight of the timeless beauty which had survived centuries of man's tribulations had rendered her problems trivial and transient, bringing with it an uplifting of her spirits. Her lethargy vanished. Some time, very soon, she vowed, she would make the tourist's obligatory pilgrimage to the 'Ancient City on the Hill', which was what 'Acropolis' meant. But first she had a duty to perform.

She went inside, showered briskly and put on the simple blue summer dress she planned to wear for her encounter with the younger generation of Mavroleons.

She roused a still sleepy Stephen and the reluctant Chryssanti and ordered breakfast for the three of them—coffee, rolls and delicious Hymettus honey.

'I don't care *what* the Mavroleons think of me,' the girl protested as Lena urged her to make the most of her appearance for her meeting with her cousins.

'Nevertheless!' Lena was firm as she brushed out the younger girl's red-gold tresses.

*   *   *

The sun was already too warm to be comfortable when they set out. Domenicos Theodopoulos had given Lena directions to the Athens office of the Mavroleon Shipping Company, and she elected to walk the short distance to the Plateia Syntagma.

Stephen was inclined to loiter. The small boy was enchanted by the many cake and sweet shops, their windows dressed with every shape and size of chocolate, Turkish delight, almond paste and nougat and an amazing variety of iced pastries. Lena hurried the child on, promising him a treat later.

Syntagma, or Constitution Square, lay on a slight slope. One side of the square faced the Parliament building where the *Evzones*, or Presidential guards, in their long white socks and shoes, kept guard, their pleated *fustanellas* swirling as they wheeled in front of the simple but impressive War Memorial.

The other three sides of the square were given over to cafés, office blocks, banks and stately hotels. Hidden away behind an airline building, and opening into an unexpected patio far from traffic noises, was the imposing suite of offices which housed the Mavroleon corporation.

Lena ushered her charges through chrome and plate-glass doors which opened into an impressive foyer with thick carpets and expensive modern furniture. It was welcomingly cool after the breathless air outside. She made enquiries of a receptionist who directed them to a private lift which carried them noiselessly to the sixth floor.

The little trio stepped out into a corridor whose carpeting seemed even thicker and more luxurious than that of the ground floor. Confronted by an impressive array of solid-looking doors, Lena paused. Then, attracted by the muffled sounds of typewriters, she selected a door, knocked and entered.

This was evidently the typing pool. An older woman, the supervisor, asked Lena's business.

'I'd like to see Mr Mavroleon.'

'Kyrios Marcos, Kyrios Christos, Kyrios Dimitri or Kyrios Manoli?'

Lena hesitated. Her information about the Mavroleon family was very sketchy. The decision was made for her.

'In any case, Kyrios Marcos and Kyrios Dimitri are out. I will ask Kyrios Christos's secretary if he can see you. What is your business?'

'It's personal,' Lena said firmly.

A moment or two later a statuesque brunette ushered them into a large, luxuriously appointed office.

'Thespinis?' A tall, dark young man of lean build rose from behind a large desk. 'How may I help you?' Keen eyes took in Chryssanti's red-gold youth, Stephen, dark and sturdy, and rested in thoughtful appreciation on Lena herself, petite, blonde and lissomely lovely. His mouth widened into a sparkling white smile.

'It's really Mr Thalassios Mavroleon I want to see,' Lena explained.

'My grandfather?' The smile faded and dark eyebrows rose enquiringly. 'My grandfather no longer takes an active part in business.'

'I realise that. Mr Theo...' Just in time, she remembered Domenicos's injunction. 'Someone told me he'd retired. But this is personal. It concerns his daughter, Irini.'

'Aunt Irini?' Christos Mavroleon's expression was wary now. 'Her name is not spoken in my grandfather's home.'

Chryssanti drew breath in a sharp hiss.

'Irini is ill,' Lena said quickly, forestalling any outburst the girl might have contemplated. 'These are her children.' She introduced the stolid, solemn-eyed Stephen and the slightly sulky-looking Chryssanti.

'*You* are a Mavroleon?' Christos said wonderingly, looking again at her bright head.

'My name is Chrys Forster,' the girl corrected defiantly. 'I prefer to be called Chrys. It sounds more English. I'm only *half-Greek*.' She made it sound as if she regretted even that half.

'Why have you brought Irini's children here?' Christos Mavroleon asked Lena, and as she hesitated, unwilling to speak more plainly in front of Stephen, Chryssanti again rushed into speech.

'She's brought us here because my mother is probably going to die and wants us to meet our grandfather. I can't think why.' She choked on a sob. 'I didn't want to come and I don't care if I *don't* meet him. He sounds a horrid old man.' The girl was crying now, tears cascading down her cheeks. She pulled at Lena's arm. 'Let's go home.' Her voice rose an octave and Stephen's lower lip began to tremble ominously. 'They don't *want* us here.'

'Chrys!' Lena protested.

'*Thespinis* Thomas, I think it would be best...' Christos was beginning, his voice raised to make itself heard, when there was an interruption which silenced them all, even Chryssanti's noisy sobs.

'*Theos mou!* Silence! All of you! Christos, explain this uproar.'

The man who erupted out of the adjoining office was an older, more striking counterpart of Christos Mavroleon. But he was taller, broader, his cleft chin was squarer, his full-lipped mouth firmer—a hint of passion warring now with impatience. Christos seemed relieved to see him.

'Marcos! I didn't know you were back.'

'Evidently!' Marcos Mavroleon's deep, rather attractive voice had a cutting edge to it. Arms akimbo, legs straddled, he filled the doorway. Lena couldn't help noticing how the excellent cut of his suit accentuated his very masculine attributes, the heavy cream linen setting off the olive texture of his skin, the long-lashed dark eyes.

'*Thespinis* Thomas,' Christos introduced hurriedly, 'this is my cousin Marcos, the senior partner of our corporation.'

Gleaming black eyes assessed Lena, missing nothing of her appearance, from the top of her wavy blonde head to the tips of her strappy white sandals. There was nothing overtly offensive in his scrutiny. Yet, with an unusual loss of her normal poise, Lena felt that the black eyes, idly contemplative, were denuding her of the peacock-blue dress with its demure white collar.

'Marcos,' his cousin went on, '*Thespinis* Thomas had brought to us the children of our Aunt Irini. Irini...' He paused, with an almost imperceptible glance at Stephen and Chryssanti. 'Irini is sick.'

The disconcerting black eyes snapped into focus.

'Irini's children? These?' He turned his attention first to Stephen, the child still uncertain whether to join in his sister's noisy grief, then to Chryssanti's tear-stained, mutinous beauty. *'Epiph!'* he breathed the curse. Then, 'You, Miss Thomas, come into my office. You...' his gaze commanded Stephen and Chryssanti '...will remain here!' He turned on his heel, a man who called the tune and expected others to dance to it.

Oddly shaken by this whirlwind encounter, Lena cast an appealing glance at Christos, but there was no help from that quarter. A nod of his dark head indicated that she should follow his cousin. On legs become suddenly tremulous, she did so. It was anger at Marcos Mavroleon's high-handed peremptory manner that was making her tremble so, she told herself.

Even from the rear he contrived to intimidate. Thick, black curly hair grew low on his strong neck. Broad-shouldered, narrow-hipped, long-legged, his very walk was a statement of arrogance.

Deliberately Lena dragged her eyes away from their compulsive assessment, concentrating instead on her surroundings.

As it befitted his status, the senior partner's office was even more magnificently appointed than that of his cousin. The carpet was thicker, the desk larger. Lena often thought that if she had not taken a degree in business studies she might have chosen to do fine arts. As it was, in her spare time, she had made a study of the history of art and she could swear that the French Impressionist paintings on the far wall were originals.

'Miss Thomas!' Marcos spun a swivel chair to face her. One hand remained steadying his chair, the other gestured her to take a seat.

Reluctantly Lena lowered herself into the soft leather depths. Instead of moving away as she had hoped, his overpowering presence continued to dominate her. She was forced to tilt her head a long way to look up at his as he loomed, very large and silently inscrutable, his eyes continuing their assessment of her.

'I'm sorry if you were disturbed,' she said, seeking to gain the initiative. 'Chrys is a very sensitive girl, and naturally she's very worried about her mother.'

'Yes—her mother,' Marcos interrupted. 'I presume you have proof that these *are* Irini's children?'

'Of course.' Lena opened her handbag and took out an envelope containing the relevant birth certificates. She watched as he subjected them to an intent scrutiny. Without comment, he returned them to her. Slightly needled by his attitude, Lena enquired 'Satisfied?'

'Thank you, yes. A wealthy family has to protect itself against impostors.' And, with scarcely a pause for breath, 'What is *your* connection with my aunt?'

Lena's fair skin coloured easily. She flushed now from neck to brow, taking his words as an implication that *she* might be a fortune hunter.

'I'm a paid employee,' she told him crisply. 'My task is to deliver Irini's children to her father. My interest ends there.'

'You are not an English relation?' he persisted. 'Of Irini's husband, perhaps?'

'No.'

He relaxed a little, she thought.

'How serious *is* Irini's illness?'

'I'm told she's unlikely to recover.'

'Who has told you this? Her husband?'

'No, her husband's dead. A friend of the family told me.' She was relieved when he did not demand further details. Instead he continued to study her in a way that did nothing to dispel her high colour, originally that of indignation, now that of embarrassment.

'You look very young to act as escort in a foreign country,' he said just as his scrutiny was becoming unbearable.

Lena's chin tilted. She was used to countering remarks like that.

'I'm twenty-five, older than I look.'

He made an incomprehensible sound and Lena stiffened as he said, 'In any event, your responsibility is ended. You have delivered your charges.'

'No!' At his enquiring look, she went on, 'My brief is to deliver Stephen and Chrys to their grandfather, no one else. Irini was very specific about that.'

His heavy brows drew together in a frown.

'Impossible!'

'I don't see why. Your grandfather *is* still alive?'

He gave a brief crack of laughter. 'Very much so.'

'Well, then!'

'My grandfather is a very private man these days. He doesn't receive visitors.'

'Visitors! Surely family doesn't come under that heading?' And, as he remained silent, 'Can't you at least get in touch and ask him?' She gestured towards the telephone.

'There is no telephone in my grandfather's home. I told you, he likes his privacy.'

'Mr Mavroleon, I suspect, for some reason of your own—goodness knows what—you're being deliberately obstructive. Can you really take it upon yourself,' she challenged him, 'to deny Irini's children access to their grandfather? If he heard of it when it was too late, are you sure he'd approve of your actions?'

'Miss Thomas,' he sounded a little weary now, 'my grandfather is not in Athens.'

'That doesn't matter. I'm prepared to go anywhere.'

'Really?' he drawled. 'But perhaps you don't realise just what that entails?'

'Mr Mavroleon!' Lena was becoming irritated. She stood up. 'When someone gives me a job to do, I do it properly, whatever inconvenience it causes.' Then, indignantly, 'What's so funny?'

CHAPTER TWO

IF ANYONE had asked her, Lena would have said that right now she was far from being susceptible to any man's charms. Petros's image was still too vivid, herself too determinedly impervious to any further risk of hurt. Yet, when she wrote the first letter to Sally that evening, her friend might have been forgiven for thinking otherwise.

'Marcos Mavroleon is tall and dark,' she wrote, 'with thick blue-black hair, very strong, rugged features, not handsome exactly, but very compelling all the same. He's got the most penetrating eyes and the deep husky kind of voice that makes your toes curl. At first sight he's a bit alarming, and he's certainly used to having his own way. I hadn't known him more than ten minutes before he was *organising* me! But when he smiles his whole face changes and you feel he might be a likeable man after all.' There was a final throw-away line, too, that perhaps revealed more than Lena realised. 'Of course his cousin Christos is very attractive, too.'

Yet, at first, when Marcos seemed to be laughing at her, Lena was angry.

'What's so funny?' she repeated. 'I meant what I said.'

'I'm sure you did, Miss Thomas. I was merely reflecting that the inconvenience you mention will be mine rather than yours.'

'I don't understand.'

To her relief he finally moved away from her chair and leaned instead against his desk, arms folded, legs crossed. The attitude drew the light-coloured material of his trousers taut across long, muscular thighs that were on a level with Lena's eyes. She found this exaggeration of his masculinity disconcerting, but in averting her gaze she met his amused one, and she was uncomfortably aware that he had noticed the hurried jerk of her head and correctly interpreted the reason for it.

'Then I will explain. There is an unusually dogged determination about you for so small a woman. Something tells me you will indeed insist on seeing my grandfather.' His smile widened, displaying impossibly perfect white teeth. 'It should be an interesting encounter.'

Lena leant forward eagerly, her vivid little face lighting up.

'Then you'll tell me where I can find him?'

'I shall myself escort you.'

'*That's* what you meant by inconvenience!' she exclaimed. 'But there's no need. I'm perfectly capable...'

'Of that I am certain,' he told her, 'but it will be my pleasure—my very great pleasure.' His black eyes glittered with a strange light.

Lena looked at him doubtfully. Was he attempting to chat her up? She had always understood that Greek men respected women and refrained from annoying them as other Mediterranean men did. But at times Marcos Mavroleon's gaze had been frankly, sexually appraising. She knew that many Greek men were attracted by the novelty of a blonde woman, so different from their own dark-complexioned beauties. For Petros the novelty had worn off, she thought with a cynicism that had once been foreign to her nature.

As she wondered about Marcos, he pressed a button on the intercom system on his desk. A husky female voice answered. He spoke in Greek, but Lena knew enough of the language to understand the sense if not the exact wording.

'Lydia, what appointments do I have in the next few days?'

The female voice rattled off a long list too quickly for Lena to follow, and Marcos listened, his dark head cocked attentively to one side. Absently Lena noticed a few silver strands amid the glossy black, just above his left ear. Somehow the flaw in the perfection made him even more attractive. Her study of his profile extended to his square, clean-cut jawline and strongly corded neck. As he spoke she watched, fascinated by the smooth ripple of his Adam's apple beneath the olive skin. His face and neck were already blue-shadowed by a strong growth of hair. He probably had to shave several times a day, she reflected. His skin would be tinglingly rough to the touch.

So vivid was the imagined sensation that she forgot to be wary in her scrutiny of him, and he turned, catching her off guard.

As she coloured once more he smiled and, furious with herself, she believed she could read his mind. He probably thought he'd made a hit with her—conceited devil!

'I find I cannot leave Athens for at least two days. After that I am at your disposal.'

'I don't see why I have to wait for you,' Lena protested.

'It is quite simple.' Again his flashing smile seemed to mock her. 'Since I shall not tell you where to find my grandfather, you can do nothing without me. And do not think,' as involuntarily she looked towards the communicating door, 'that Christos or any of my cousins will enlighten you without my permission. And now,' before she could draw breath for an indignant exclamation, 'let us think how you are to fill the next day or so. At what hotel are you staying?'

'I'm not. I have the use of a friend's flat.' He waited, patently expecting more, but she wasn't about to elaborate. 'And we can take the opportunity to do some sightseeing.'

'The boy is a little young to drag around in this heat,' Marcos commented. 'May I make a suggestion?'

Could she prevent him? Lena thought wryly. Could a rowing-boat prevent the progress of one of his oil tankers?

'My aunt Anastasia, Christos's mother, has a villa just outside the city. Stefanos and Chryssanti could spend a few days with her, leaving you free to come and go as you please.'

Lena shook her head. 'Stephen, yes, Chrys, no. She'd better stay with me.'

'Ah, I see. You are afraid the Mavroleons will spirit the two of them away and deprive you of the satisfaction of doing your duty.'

Until he said this, the idea hadn't crossed her mind. She might have her doubts about Marcos Mavroleon's bold, assessing gaze, but in other matters she felt instinctively he was to be trusted, and instinct rarely played her false. Except in the case of Petros Theodopoulos, she reminded herself, and a little stab of pain made her grimace.

'I have hit the nail on the head, no?'

'Not at all,' she told him. 'It's just that Chrys is here very much against her will. She's afraid and resentful. She might be discourteous to your aunt. Besides, whether she likes it or not, Greece *is* her inheritance. It might be a good thing for her to appreciate some of its beauties, its history.'

'I see you are not only an attractive young woman, but a wise one.' And as Lena blushed, he went on, 'So be it.' With a glance at his watch which revealed a wrist strongly coated with dark, virile hair, he said, 'It is too late now, but tomorrow I will take you to meet my aunt, so you may satisfy yourself of her suitability to care for Stefanos.'

'His name is Stephen,' Lena reminded him, and he shrugged.

'It is the same thing, and to me the Greek name comes more easily.' He straightened and moved towards the door, held it wide open. It was a dismissal, and Lena found herself automatically complying.

In the outer office peace now reigned. Christos had sent out for ice-cream for his young cousins. Stephen, with besmeared hands and face, grinned beatifically at Lena. But Christos had recognised that Chryssanti was no longer a child to be placated with sticky treats, and the two of them were deep in conversation. Chryssanti was actually smiling.

'Until tomorrow then, Miss Thomas.' Marcos came no further than the threshold of his office.

'What's happening tomorrow?' Chryssanti asked on the lift's downward journey and, when Lena explained, 'Why can't *Christos* take us to meet his mother? I like *him*.'

'I'm sure you'll like *all* your cousins when you get to know them,' Lena reassured her, unconsciously defending Marcos.

Lena had insisted that she would bring her charges to the Mavroleon office next morning. She couldn't risk giving Marcos her Athens address, in case he knew who owned the building. She deplored the need for such cloak and dagger behaviour, but Domenicos had been insistent that his name should not be brought into her dealings with Irini's family.

She'd taken considerable trouble this morning, not just over Chryssanti's and Stephen's appearance, but over her own. The Greeks, she had found, were hospitable people. Nevertheless, it was an honour to be invited into the private home of someone she'd never met, a wealthy home moreover, and she felt she must do justice to the surroundings.

She hadn't dressed for *his* benefit. Nevertheless, she was aware of the approbation in Marcos's eyes as they took in her slight but perfectly proportioned figure, enhanced by the cut of the cream silk skirt and jacket with the toning coffee-coloured blouse. She had wondered a little at the advisability of wearing the high-heeled sandals that matched the outfit. She had several pairs of flat shoes. But somehow she felt the need to minimise her lack of inches. Marcos Mavroleon was so dauntingly tall.

His chauffeur-driven limousine, fitted out with every luxury, including a telephone, was ready and they left immediately, following the road that ran out of Athens and past the airport. Their route then hugged the shore, twisting in and out along a succession of bays where blue seas broke on golden sands.

It was around midday when the limousine turned inland and took a steep twisting road, thick with white dust, that ran up into the heat-shimmered hills. Far below, white villas among sombre trees dotted the grey coast and, on a promontory lunging out into the blue Aegean, Lena caught a glimpse of white columns glittering in the sunlight—a temple?

'The temple of Poseidon,' Marcos confirmed in answer to her eager question.

'The God of the Sea.'

'You are familiar with our gods and goddesses?'

'Yes, I've always been interested in anything to do with Greece.'

Wishing they might have gone closer, Lena craned her neck until the temple was lost to sight.

'Greece has many temples, Miss Thomas. By the time you leave you will have had a surfeit of them.'

'I doubt it,' she told him. 'Can one ever have enough of beauty?'

'Perhaps not.' But his bold black eyes lingered on her face rather than on the scenery. 'I think a man might look at *you* for a long time, Miss Thomas.'

Lena was used to receiving compliments. There were many ways of dealing with them, depending upon the sincerity or otherwise of the donor. But somehow this time she found herself unable to make a coherent reply either of thanks or of humorous self-deprecation. She'd never met anyone quite like Marcos Mavroleon before. And yet why? He had the same component parts as any other attractive male. In fact, in her time she'd met handsomer men. So why this unusual discomposure?

Anastasia Mavroleon was a charming hostess, a dark woman with quiet and delicate movements. Lena liked her immediately and she felt no compunction about leaving Stephen in the older woman's care. To her surprise, when given a choice, Chryssanti too opted for remaining at the villa for the next few days.

'I've never liked sightseeing,' she told Lena. 'You'll enjoy it much better without me.'

That was probably true, and Lena had never minded her own company—until she'd met Petros, she reminded herself, and become accustomed to being a twosome. But it was a good thing that Chryssanti now seemed disposed to make an effort to get on with her Greek relations. What did disconcert Lena was the thought of travelling back to Athens alone with Marcos Mavroleon. One couldn't count the chauffeur, isolated behind the limousine's thick dividing glass panel.

'You have never visited Greece before?'

She was grateful when, on the return journey, Marcos initiated the conversation. She wasn't usually so stupidly tongue-tied.

'No. But I'd always meant to some day.'

'That's why you took on the task of escorting Irini's children?'

'Partly.'

'You had some other reason for wishing to leave England?'

'Not one I want to discuss.' But he was too perceptive.

'A broken romance?' he hazarded.

'Yes, if you must know. But I said I didn't . . .'

'What foolish man would allow *you* to escape him?' Marcos mused.

'Please, there's no need to . . .'

'To flatter you?' His dark eyes viewed her flushed confusion with deep interest. 'Believe me, that was not my intention. Flattery is so often insincere. But you must know that you are a very lovely young woman.' To her relief, he did not pursue the theme. Instead he leant forward and slid open the glass partition, giving the chauffeur rapid instructions in his own language.

They were approaching the bend in the road from which Lena had glimpsed the Temple of Poseidon, and to her surprise the limousine left the main road, following instead a twisting offshoot out on to the headland.

'This is a favourite target for the tourist coaches.' Marcos seemed to be apologising for the fact, and Lena realised why when she saw the restaurant with its crowded car park and the array of tables outside, set under brightly coloured umbrellas.

'We will walk a little way up the hillside,' Marcos decided. And with a wry glance at Lena's sandals, 'You will need more appropriate footwear for your sightseeing.'

'Yes, I realise that. But I wasn't expecting...'

'You looked so wistful as we passed by on our way this morning, I found myself wishing to gratify your curiosity.' He took her arm to guide her over the worn track that led up to the promontory. Lena tried to tell herself that his hold was an impersonal one, but found herself disturbed by it all the same.

Whatever is the matter with you? she scolded herself. You've just been discarded by one man. Just because you're lonely, don't for heaven's sake do anything foolish like falling for another one on the rebound. Anyway, you only met him twenty-four hours ago. You know nothing about him. He could be married... She realised that Marcos was speaking and forced herself to pay attention.

'The temple was built in the Great Age, under Pericles. It is made of pure white marble. Originally it had nineteen columns. Only twelve are left.'

Lena wished they could have climbed right up to the summit, but even at this distance it was an impressive sight. Its beauty lay as much in its situation as in its architectural form. To either side of it the coast fell away, so that the temple dominated the scene for many miles around. Beyond it, inland, the green slopes of olive groves and vineyards merged into dark, uncultivable land broken by stony outcrops. And beyond again rose rocky heights, sharply outlined against the clear, burning blue sky. The rugged grandeur of the scene must differ very little from what it had been in the days of the ancient Greeks. The beauty of it caught at Lena's heart, and impulsively she looked up into Marcos's face.

'Thank you for bringing me here.'

He inclined his dark head.

'It is my pleasure. In fact, I should like to show you more of our national treasures. I tend to take them for granted. It is refreshing to see them in the company of one so appreciative.'

She found herself waiting expectantly, and was aware of irrational disappointment when he said no more. Of course, she told herself, as they returned in silence to the limousine, he was only being polite. There was no reason why either of them should seek the other's company. It was only her errand that had brought them together.

So it was with pleased surprise that she heard him issue an invitation to dine with him that evening. She felt bound to utter a disclaimer.

'You mustn't feel obliged to entertain *me*.'

'Oh, but I *shall* feel obliged—if you accept!'

He was doing it again, disconcerting her with the liquid gaze of those dark eyes, the husky intonation of his voice, and if she had any sense she'd refuse politely. But common sense seemed in unusually short supply. After all, there was no reason why she shouldn't enjoy herself. She might still be in love with Petros Theodopoulos, but she owed him no loyalty. And though she'd disagreed with Sally at the time, maybe the way to forget one man *was* to find another. Not that she was planning on anything more than a pleasant holiday association. And

there was still that unanswered question in her mind—
was he married? She approached the subject as closely
as she dared.

'It might not be convenient to . . . to your family. You
may be expected at home.'

'There will be no inconvenience. I live alone.'

'You will forgive me if I send you home unescorted?'
Marcos asked as the limousine paused briefly outside
the Mavroleon office.

'I can walk from here,' she told him hastily. 'It isn't
far to my flat.' But Marcos signalled to the chauffeur
to drive on, and she found herself having to direct the
man through the crowded streets. Though still slightly
bemused by the events of the day, Lena had wit enough
to tell him to stop two blocks from her own.

'I will pick you up at seven this evening, *thespinis*,'
the chauffeur called after her.

Lena spun on her heel, but it was too late. Already
the limousine was gliding away. Damn, that was the
trouble with having to dissemble. Now she'd have to be
on this spot tonight if she wanted to keep her date with
Marcos. And she did want to, very much.

As she considered the contents of her wardrobe that
evening, Lena thanked heaven for her experience of
mingling with wealthy friends of her Greek employer.
True, she hadn't expected to do much socialising while
in Athens, but she had packed one or two dressy outfits,
just in case.

She had no idea where they would be going, but the
silky-look wrapover dress in a sumptuous burgundy-
coloured Persian print was suitable for most occasions.
She donned matching burgundy tights and shoes, and
the heavy gold necklace and earrings which had been her

last birthday present from Petros. Left to herself, she would never have purchased anything quite so expensive, but they were just the thing for tonight.

She knew that even in summer Greek evenings could be cool, and as she left the flat she threw a light jacket around her shoulders.

Guessing that anyone who worked for Marcos Mavroleon would be punctual, she timed her arrival to coincide exactly with that of the limousine. If the chauffeur was surprised to see her already standing outside, he did not show it.

Lena was a little surprised and, yes, a little piqued that Marcos had not called for her himself. She was even more surprised and a little dismayed when the chauffeur took her, not to a restaurant, but to an elegant private house in the modern part of the city.

A thin-faced, severe-looking woman admitted her and showed her into a large salon, then, with a few muttered words in a tone that seemed to imply disapproval, left her to her own devices.

Lena had spent the last few hours since her parting with Marcos telling herself she had no need to be so nervous about seeing him again. But it was an apprehension that mingled with anticipation. Now, in his house, the tremulous excitement had returned. But this time she wasn't going to allow nerves to betray the startling effect he had on her. She would be calm, friendly, but coolly so. To steady herself, she began an appraisal of the room in which she waited.

As she would have expected, nothing that wealth or good taste could provide was lacking. Thick wall-to-wall carpeting, glowing antique furniture, subtly lit paintings—Picasso, Manet, Lautrec and others were among those she could identify. She was on the point of moving closer to study the brushwork when the door behind her opened, and despite all her resolutions she started violently.

In evening dress Marcos Mavroleon was even more striking, in a way that made her blood race. He came towards her, holding out his hand. She swallowed and strove for a steady tone as she put her fingers into his.

'Mr Mavroleon, you have a lovely home. I was admiring your paintings.'

'You are interested in art?' And at her nod, 'Then you will enjoy my grandfather's collection. Compared with his, mine is very modest.' He released her hand but only to slide his beneath her elbow, his fingers warm on her bare flesh. He guided her towards large double doors at the end of the salon, and she found herself in a small intimate dining-room. The table was set for two, the places not opposite but adjacent at one corner. 'I hope you do not mind dining here, *à deux*,' he said, continuing smoothly before she could reply 'After a long day, I find it more restful to eat at home.'

Courteously, he seated her at the table, a process which brought him once more into close proximity, with an unsettling effect upon her nerves. Lena had expected a bevy of servants, but he helped her himself from a side table.

'I thought you might not be accustomed to our food,' he observed as he offered her a choice between a chicken salad and freshly cooked fish. 'So I asked my chef to prepare a simple meal.'

In fact Lena was quite used to Greek cooking and very fond of it, but she thought it best not to enlighten him. If Domenicos Theodopoulos's name was to be kept out of this, the less Marcos knew about her background, the better. She was very much afraid anyway that he was going to question her about herself, and she searched her brain frantically for a topic that would divert him and last throughout the meal.

'Tell me something about your grandfather,' she said as he sat down.

The black eyes were quizzical. 'What do you want to know?'

She hadn't expected the conversational ball to be returned so smartly to her court, and she fumbled a little for words.

'Basically the sort of person he is, I suppose. Whether or not he's likely to accept his grandchildren.'

'He has a very strong sense of family, of course,' Marcos said slowly. 'But in return he demands loyalty, the observance of tradition. Irini's elopement caused him a great deal of embarrassment among his social equals.'

'That's not the children's fault.'

'True. Tell me, Miss Thomas, what do Irini's children ask of my grandfather?'

This was not the line she'd hoped the conversation would take, but she struggled to give an answer.

'Stephen is too young to understand why he's here,' she pointed out. 'Chrys says she doesn't even want to meet him. She sees him as a tyrant, I'm afraid, and she's hot in defence of her mother.'

'Then let me put my question another way. What does my aunt ask of her father? Money? The inheritance that would have been hers if she had not estranged herself from her family?'

Lena shook her head.

'Irini's not hard up. Her husband left her very well provided for and his parents are very fond of Irini. Mr and Mrs Forster had no other children, so presumably Stephen and Chryssanti will be their heirs.'

'They are wealthy?'

'Moderately—nothing to compare with the Mavroleon millions, of course.' She was joking. She had no idea what Marcos and his family were worth, but if the Theodopoulos Company was to be taken as a measure of wealth...

'So you have done your homework!' His face was stern suddenly. 'What else do you know about my family?' He sounded almost accusing, as if he believed her interest to be one of cupidity.

'I think you misunderstand, Mr Mavroleon.' Lena could be abrupt too if she felt her probity was under attack. 'I know absolutely nothing about your family, and for myself I'm not really interested. My remark was meant as a joke. As far as I'm concerned, there are more important things in life than money.'

He raised a cynical eyebrow, and his expression irritated her.

'Oh, I know you Greeks think making money is the be all and end all, but...'

'You *know* this?' he enquired smoothly. 'Tell me more.'

Lena shook her head, regretting her outburst. She mustn't be drawn into revealing her wide acquaintance with Greek businessmen.

'That's not what we're discussing. You asked what Irini wanted of her father. I'll tell you what she told me. She never stopped loving her father, even though she went against him in the matter of her marriage.'

'She regretted this marriage?'

'Certainly not. It was a happy, successful marriage. But even so she always felt a certain sadness. She was deprived of affectionate contact with her father. But it was a two-way thing. He had lost a daughter. By sending her children to their grandfather, she's hoping to make amends before she dies, hoping he can give *them* the love denied her and vice versa.'

Lena was entirely caught up in what she was saying, in the vivid memory of Irini's face, wan with ill-health, sad with recollection. She remembered the tears the other woman had let fall as she spoke of her father and her homeland, and her own blue eyes were full and brilliant as she concluded her impassioned speech.

Marcos seemed convinced and impressed too, for he leaned forward and rested his hand on hers.

'You make a good advocate, Miss Thomas. Tell me, are all your emotions as strong as these?' He paused and his voice became subtly deeper. 'Do you love as deeply as you feel for the misfortunes of others?' And as she did not reply. 'Miss Thomas...' He broke off with an irritated gesture. '*Theos mou!* I cannot keep up this ridiculous formality. *You* will call *me* Marcos.' The pressure of his hand increased. 'And *your* name?'

Lena had clung to formality as a barrier against the attraction he held for her. Now, reluctantly, she told him, 'Lena. Short for Helena,' she explained as his brow wrinkled over the unfamiliar form.

'Ah!' His expression lightened. '*That* I like. I shall call you Helena. It is a Greek name, you know. Have you any Greek blood?' She shook her head. 'But you have heard of Helen of Troy? It is fitting that you share her name. "Is this,"' he declaimed suddenly, '"the face that launched a thousand ships?"'

No doubt he intended it as a compliment, but Lena was suddenly reduced to a fit of most unromantic giggles. At his look of puzzled outrage the giggles threatened to become worse. But he was obviously unused to being laughed at in this fashion. With difficulty she mastered herself.

'I'm s-sorry!' she gasped. 'I'm not laughing at *you*. It's just that when I was at school the boys used to tease me about my name. I was a very plump child—oh, yes,' in reply to his grunt of disbelief, 'and they used to mis-quote that saying—"Is this the face that lunched a thousand chips?"'

He wouldn't understand, of course, she thought in the momentary pause that followed but it seemed his English *was* equal to making the connection, for he broke into delighted laughter, his face creasing into a dozen attractive lines. He murmured the words over to himself.

'This I must remember. But,' he sobered and his black eyes were eloquent, 'they could not say this of you now, Helena. So slender, so chic, so very, very lovely.'

The compliments were coming a little too thick and fast for her liking, Lena thought uncomfortably, and his hand still rested on hers. Carefully she withdrew it. De-liberately prosaic, she observed, 'This fish is really very good.'

He made a noise in his throat that sounded like one of irritation. With her eyes fixed steadily on her meal, she waited a little nervously for an explosion of wrath. But it did not come. Instead he too went on eating. After a moment he asked, 'What would you like us to do tomorrow?'

'Tomorrow?' In surprise she looked up from her plate. 'Us?' And as he nodded, 'I wasn't expecting... You're busy. Your appointments. Your secretary said...'

'You understand Greek?' He was down on her remark like a flash.

'Not really, just a few words. Enough to know...'

'My appointments have to be kept. But they will not take me all day. So! Tomorrow?'

Lena gestured helplessly.

'There's so much. Museums, I suppose, the Acropolis...'

'Ah, yes, the Acropolis. But you do not want to see this for the first time by day, with a thousand others. The time to see it is at night.' He pushed back his chair and moved over to the side table. He brought her a dish of creamy yoghurt liberally sprinkled with nuts and honey. '*I* will take you there tonight.'

'Oh, but...'

'It will be my pleasure,' he said with the masterful air of finality she was beginning to recognise.

Like the prow of an enormous ship, the Acropolis soared above the roofs of the city. On all sides but one its cliffs rose a sheer five hundred feet high. Floodlights played not only on its cliffs, but also on its temples, making it appear a phantom city of palaces high in the night sky, a worthy dwelling for the gods.

'Forget everything you have read,' Marcos had told Lena. 'To the insensitive, the Acropolis is little more than a pile of ruins. To a romantic, it is a memorial to all that is fine about Greece and her people.'

Marcos had his chauffeur drop them off below the southern face so that they could walk up the steep ascent, then climb the giant staircase to the Propylaea, the gateway to the Acropolis. From the plateau, a splendid panoramic view lay before them. One hand resting on her shoulder, with the other Marcos pointed out in turn the distant mountains of Argolis, Piraeus and the islands of Salamis, Aegina and Poros, the blue waters of the Gulf, and Mount Hymettus, famous for its honey, its slopes now flushed deep violet in the aftermath of sunset.

Lena breathed deeply, a sigh of appreciation. Here, high above the city, the air was a heady blend of pine from the hills, ozone from the sea, jasmine from a thousand balconies and courtyards. Beauty, in any form, always had the power to move her—unbearably, sometimes. It was difficult to put her feelings into words. But she might have tried, she thought, had she been with someone she knew really well. Once, she'd thought to share scenes like this with Petros. Instead she was here with this admittedly attractive stranger, and it was foolish to suppose he could ever be more than that. Her eyes blurred as a great sense of loneliness engulfed her.

'What are you thinking?' Marcos asked suddenly, the touch of his hand startling her into an unguarded reply.

'How sad it is that nothing lasts.'

'The Acropolis has lasted for many thousands of years.' He sounded puzzled.

'I meant people, relationships.'

'Ah, you are thinking of the broken romance? What was he like, this man, I wonder? You are feeling sad because you still love him?' Subtly his voice had changed, and her heartbeat increased its tempo as his hand tightened on her shoulder. She swallowed. 'You still love him?' Marcos repeated.

'I suppose so,' she whispered a little breathlessly. But she wasn't at all sure what it was she was feeling right now.

CHAPTER THREE

FOR some part of each of the days that followed, Lena
explored alone. But she found herself looking forward
more and more to the hours she spent with Marcos, when
he could spare the time, seeing more of Athens and
learning a little more about the enigmatic man who had
constituted himself as her guide. She had known him
for such a short time, and yet everything about him ex-
cited her.

However, she was more than a little puzzled by
Marcos's attitude towards her. He still continued to pay
her compliments, and she had no doubt they were
genuine. At times she could have sworn the sexual attraction *she* felt was mutual. But, every time she sensed
he was about to make some move towards greater intimacy, he seemed suddenly to withdraw into himself.

On the occasions when she attempted to question him
about his grandfather, he remained evasive. Even so, she
gained the impression that Thalassios Mavroleon was still
very much the autocrat, ruling his family with a rod of
iron.

'My grandfather saw to it that I went to your Oxford
University and had a training in business administration
before he allowed me to become his *aide*. My cousins he
sent to school in Paris. They all speak French. No Greek
is considered well educated unless he can speak at least
one other language.'

For all his wealth, Marcos Mavroleon was capable of
enjoying himself at a simple level.

They talked endlessly about art and their favourite books, late at night in the fashionable heart of the city, seated in a carefully preserved replica of a Greek village *cafenion*. There were a few other foreigners around, Lena noted, but mostly there were Greeks, sipping endless cups of their beloved thick black coffee with the inevitable accompanying glasses of water. They visited some of the best examples of Byzantine churches as well as the major museums. But, because it was Lena's favourite they went again and again to the Acropolis, seeing it in all conditions of light—the pearly pink reflection of early morning, the brazen glare of shimmering noon, the gentle peach and purple glow of sunset and the mysterious shadows of bright moonlight.

'I shall always connect you with this place,' Marcos told her. It was on one of the occasions when Lena had felt particularly close to him, and his words jarred unpleasantly on her. They referred to a future when she would no longer be in his company.

She still couldn't be certain whether her growing feelings for him were genuine. To Sally she wrote, 'He's an interesting man to be with. He knows so much about so many things. He has a sense of humour, too, though he doesn't laugh very often. But he's exasperatingly secretive about his family and I don't seem to be any nearer getting to see his grandfather. Yes, the more I see of Marcos, the more I like him. I know you'll probably laugh and say I'm on the rebound in spite of what I said. And you could be right, which is why I'm trying hard not to fall for him.'

As a pleasant and refreshing contrast to the dust and glare of the city, Marcos suggested they take a ferry excursion to one of the islands.

'Aegina, perhaps?' he suggested. 'The hydrofoil would be quicker, but we are in no hurry, hmm?' and Lena wished she could believe he wanted to extend his time in her company.

They drove first to Piraeus, the port of Athens for three thousand years, where ships seemed to arrive and depart every five minutes. Lena found Piraeus a noisy, rumbustious place. Taxis screeched to a halt depositing voluble passengers who shoved their way aboard the various vessels, shouting farewells to relations and friends on the quayside. Ships sirens shrieked, laughter issued from tavernas, accompanied by thin pagan strains of Greek music from an unseen radio.

There was a mad scramble for seats, and Lena guessed that without Marcos's forceful presence and the protection of his strong arm, she might not have secured one.

'Thanks!' She laughed up into his face, the sound melodious and unselfconscious. 'It's worse than a trip from Southend pier.'

He looked at her with a curiously arrested expression on his face. Then, 'You do not mind being jostled so?'

'Not a bit.'

'Many women would dislike it.'

'Not me! In the right company it's...' She stopped short, colour running up into cheeks that in the last few days had acquired a honey-gold tan.

'You were going to say?'

'It's fun,' she said lamely.

'My company is...*fun*?' With raised eyebrows, he queried the word.

'It just means I'm enjoying myself,' she explained, feeling more and more embarrassed. 'Fun means to laugh, to be happy.'

'Ah! You are *happy* with me!' She couldn't tell if he was pleased or otherwise, and she was relieved when he changed the subject.

The sea was lovely and varied in its colouring, from violet blue to rich jade greens, and the crossing was enjoyable, long enough to be refreshing, not long enough to be boring.

'Aegina,' Marcos said at last, pointing to a picture postcard mountain, sloping down to the Saronic gulf.

The little boat edged her way into the smooth waters of the delightful port—homely and traditional with its ochre-hued houses. A dazzlingly white church like a mosque stood at the end of one pier. Trawlers were moored tightly side by side in the harbour.

Ashore, they relaxed for a while in the sunlight, watching the movement in the harbour, and Lena feasted her eyes on the mountains of Poros and the ranges of hills on the Peloponnesus.

'But you have come to see history, not just scenery,' Marcos said.

A bus trip from the quayside took them to the northeast of the island to the pretty village of Messangros. On the pine-covered hill above the village stood the temple of Aphaia which was, Marcos told her, one of the most remarkable monuments of its kind in Greece. They sat among the ruins, overlooking the coastline with its long, sandy beaches and magnificent views that stretched as far as Athens.

'I love islands,' Lena said dreamily. 'I've always thought I'd like to live on an island.'

'So? But not all Greek islands are like this, Helena. Some are very remote, with no means of communication—no mail, no telephones.' His words touched a chord in Lena's memory.

'Does your grandfather by any chance live on an island?'

'Why do you ask?'

'Something you said made me think... And I've heard it said that a Greek shipowner without an island is like a king without his clothes.' She wondered for a moment if her frankness had offended him. But he gave a wry smile.

'We Greeks are used to myth and legend, even where it concerns ourselves. But in this case you are right. The Mavroleons own not just an island, but a group of them. And, yes, my grandfather does live there.'

'Tell me about the islands,' Lena begged, but he shrugged.

'In a few days you will see for yourself. That will be better than any poor description of mine.'

'We're going to see your grandfather? At last? He's given his permission?'

'We leave the day after tomorrow. But he knows nothing of our visit as yet. It is our custom in Greece to celebrate a friend or relative's name day—the feast of the saint after whom they are named. We shall visit as a family. Perhaps the occasion will make him more inclined to accept two new grandchildren.' He paused, then, 'You will find my grandfather's establishment an old-fashioned one. You may not understand or agree with all you see there.'

'I promise not to be rude enough to say so,' Lena told him, more rashly than she realised.

When Marcos had said they would visit his grandfather as a family, Lena had not envisagd just what that would entail. They drove up to Anastasia's villa to collect Stephen and Chryssanti. Stephen was his usual placid self, but the few days had wrought a miraculous change in Chryssanti Forster. She met Lena with a radiant face and a glowing smile.

'I'm so glad you left me with Aunt Tassia. She's a darling.'

But an observant Lena soon noticed that it was *Christos* Mavroleon who was responsible for the change in his cousin. Christos and his two brothers still lived with their mother, thus Chryssanti had seen him every evening. Apparently the good-natured young man had paid her a considerable amount of attention, and Lena was a little worried to realise that the impressionable girl was already fathoms deep in love with him.

They travelled down to Piraeus in two limousines, and Chryssanti insisted on accompanying Christos, his mother and his younger brother, Manoli. The older brother, Dimitri, sat in the back of Marcos's car with Stephen.

At Piraeus there were more surprises when they boarded a small launch which took them out into the harbour to where an enormous yacht, the *Poseidon*, rode at anchor on the low offshore tide, alone and regal.

'Does this yacht belong to my grandfather?' Stephen Forster put the question Lena longed to ask.

'No, to me,' Marcos told him, and to Lena, 'Come, I'll show you round.'

In a daze she followed him, from deck to deck, from dining salon to library, to the sauna, from suite to suite. On the gleaming teak of the afterdeck was a helicopter pad and a large, mosaic-tiled swimming pool which could be covered to make a dance-floor.

'It's enormous,' Lena marvelled when the tour finally ended with the suite which was to be hers and

Chryssanti's for the voyage. 'You wouldn't know you were on board ship.'

During their absence the launch had made another trip ashore, returning to the boarding stairs this time with an assortment of uncles and aunts whose individual names were too many to memorise. One of the aunts, Lena noticed, was a nun.

It was almost dusk when the great yacht weighed anchor and set sail, her sleek lines and proud bearing carrying her effortlessly over the placid sea. Marcos had left his guests while he supervised their departure and Lena found herself sitting on a sofa in one of the salons with Christos's mother.

'It's nice to see Chrys looking so much happier,' she told Anastasia. 'It was very good of you to look after her and Stephen, Kyria Mavroleon. I hope they were no trouble to you?'

'None whatsoever. But please call me Tassia, everyone else does. Chrys is a charming child and very popular with my sons. They have all been at great pains to entertain her and distract her from her grief. And you, my dear, are you enjoying your stay in Greece?'

'Very much. Marcos...' For some reason, saying his name to a member of his family made Lena blush. 'Mr Mavroleon has been very kind. I've seen so much more than if I'd been alone.'

'Yes?' Tassia Mavroleon said thoughtfully. Then, 'You like my nephew?' Her brown eyes were shrewdly observant. They had detected the betraying blush. 'My dear,' she hesitated, 'it is perhaps not my place to say anything. But as woman to woman...and you are a foreigner, unaccustomed to our ways...' She paused again, and Lena waited with an odd sinking feeling for her to continue. She had an idea Anastasia Mavroleon did not approve of her friendship with Marcos, that she was going to be warned off. She was right.

'The Mavroleons are not easy men to understand. There is much of their grandfather in them. They are all hopelessly steeped in tradition, and their name says much about their character.' And as Lena looked questioningly at her, 'Mavroleon means Black Lion. They roar, they have black moods—and the most like his grandfather is Marcos—so much so even his friends have dubbed him "The Black Lion of Skiapelos".'

'Skiapelos?'

'The name of the group of islands which are their home. Be very careful, Helena.' An expensively be-ringed finger lightly tapped Lena's cheek. 'Be advised, do not become involved, do not allow yourself to be hurt. *I* married a Mavroleon, *I* know.'

Lena had wondered about Anastasia's husband, who had not been mentioned and did not form one of the family party.

'We are divorced,' the older woman added, as if in answer to the unspoken question. 'And another thing you should remember, Helena—I am sure you are too sensible to misunderstand my nephew—but it is almost unheard of for a Mavroleon to marry a foreigner.'

Perhaps, Lena mused, that was one of the reasons why she was so attracted to Marcos, the lure of something which she had sensed for herself was unattainable.

Anastasia might have gone on to say more if Marcos had not returned to the salon at that moment. He came directly towards Lena, and she felt her heart begin to thud rapidly as it always seemed to when he was near.

'Helena, there is something I wish to show you. Come with me.' He held out his hand to pull her up from the deep sofa.

Anastasia's words might have made Lena refuse, reject his gesture. But he did not wait for any opposition, taking her slim hand in his and drawing her to his side.

'You will excuse us, Tassia!' he said to his aunt. It was not a question, but said in the manner of one who does not expect or accept opposition.

Looking at Anastasia in rueful apology, Lena caught a warning glance from the brown eyes and an almost imperceptible shake of the head. With any other man Lena knew she probably would have resisted the almost imperious invitation, might have heeded his aunt's outspoken warning. But from the moment she put her hand in his and felt the warmth of his fingers curled firmly about her own, she was lost to all caution, accompanying him gladly.

So what if her acquaintance with Marcos Mavroleon was only a transitory exaltation of the spirits? Life was a journey, not a destination, and she meant to enjoy it in all its stages. After her experience with Petros, she'd decided she wasn't looking for permanence—at least, not yet. That way, she'd already discovered, lay disappointment and unhappiness. She felt a reckless impulse to live for the present. What was it her father was always saying? 'Tomorrow may never come' and 'Today is the tomorrow you worried about yesterday'.

'Where are we going?' she asked breathlessly. She had to hurry to keep up with Marcos's long strides.

'Up on deck.' Once out of the harbour, the *Poseidon* had travelled only a short distance along the coastline to its present position. 'We shall anchor here tonight and continue our journey at first light.'

'What did you want to show me?'

'The sunset,' Marcos told her. 'Look!'

'Oh!' Lena drew a long, rapturous breath.

They leant against the railing. On the horizon the sky was a pastiche of orange, pink and deep red, melding into a darkening sea. Lena was aware of Marcos watching her, waiting for her reaction to the scene. But she was totally unaware of the picture she herself made, her long, luxuriant hair tossed by an errant sea breeze, the pure lines of her profile silhouetted against the soft glow of the sunset.

'You look like a figurehead or a classic sculpture,' he said softly. 'But a warm, living sculpture, far more lovely than any wooden or cold marble image.' There was something different about him suddenly. Previously, his compliments had been issued with an air of reserve which had detracted from their value—as a man might perhaps comment on an object of beauty he admired but could never possess.

She turned to look up at him trying to fathom the expression on his shadowed face.

He put a hand on her arm where it rested beside his on the rail.

'Helena...' His maleness was a potent presence, and there was an urgency in his tone to which something inside her responded.

'Yes?'

'There is something I have been meaning to...'

'Lena! Aunt Tassia sent me to find you.' It was Chryssanti, blithely unaware of intrusion. 'She says it's time to dress for dinner.'

Anastasia Mavroleon had done it on purpose, of course, but whether out of genuine concern for Lena's welfare or out of family loyalty Lena couldn't be sure.

'Coming, Chrys.' She hoped the younger girl would go on ahead, having delivered her message. But Chryssanti lingered and Marcos had retreated into his usual reserve. 'I . . . I'll see you later,' Lena said to his profile, and felt chilled by his curt, dismissive nod. Perhaps he was relieved at the interruption.

In their suite, Lena and Chryssanti changed, Chryssanti into a softly flowing dress in a deep sea green that accorded well with her red-gold hair and tawny eyes.

'I wish I had a more grown-up dress,' the younger girl said, looking with envy at the sophisticated but simply cut golden sheath Lena wore. 'You *are* pretty, Lena. You're sort of golden all over.'

'Thank you, Chrys. But you're pretty too, you know.'

'Do you think so? Do you think a *man* would think I'm pretty?'

By a man, Lena presumed she meant Christos, but young love was a delicate plant and she trod warily. She put an arm about the girl.

'Don't lose your heart yet, Chrys. You're still young.'

'It's too late.' There was a quaint yet pathetic maturity about the girl that tugged at Lena's sympathies. 'I think Christos is wonderful. I don't care what anyone says.'

'What *have* people been saying?'

'Oh, Manoli and Dimitri have been trying to put me off him, especially Dimitri. I can't *stand* Dimitri Mavroleon.' Then, with a sudden change of mood. 'Lena, if . . . if Mum dies, will Stephen and I be staying in Greece?'

'I don't know, dear. It depends on your grandfather, I suppose.'

'Because . . . because I wouldn't mind staying *too* much.' The words 'because of Christos' were not stated, but they were implied. 'So long as I can visit Nan and Gramps Forster sometimes. They'll miss me and Stephen.'

As they made their way to the dining salon, Lena breathed a quick prayer that things would work out happily for Chryssanti. Already she was fond of the girl and her small brother. She would have added a rider to the prayer on her own behalf, if she'd been quite sure what it was she wanted.

The Mavroleon women were beautifully dressed. Some were in white with flowing Grecian lines. The older women favoured black. Together their jewellery must amount to a small fortune. Lena felt decidedly underdressed, unaware that the simplicity of her outfit, her youthful beauty, needed no extra adornment.

Marcos was at the head of the table, an elderly uncle on his right, the nun on his left. The rest of the family seated themselves according to some unspoken but obviously familiar protocol. Lena and her charges were at the bottom of the pecking order.

During her acquaintance with the Theodopouloses, Lena had become accustomed to their opulent life-style. But, as she ate off Meissen plates, used heavy silver cutlery and drank out of crystal glasses, she was beginning to realise they were not in the same league as the Mavroleons.

Chryssanti, next to Christos, was happy, all smiles and sparkling eyes. She was openly flirting with her handsome cousin. Lena was half amused, half concerned. But perhaps this was what Irini Forster had had in mind, she thought: that Chryssanti should marry one of her cousins and be accepted back into the fold that her mother had fled.

Distanced though she was from Marcos, Lena found her eyes constantly straying to where he sat, very much assured in his position as host. Evening dress suited him, the impeccable whiteness of his shirt front setting off his swarthy attractiveness. He seemed deeply engaged in conversation with his elderly relatives, and yet, when Lena glanced his way, invariably she met his speculative stare. Once, he raised his glass to her, an imperceptible gesture perhaps unnoticed by anyone else.

But yes, Anastasia had noticed. Her expression was grave and Lena flushed, resolving from now on to keep her wayward eyes firmly fixed on her plate, her attention on her more immediate neighbours. But even though she managed to restrain her eyes, she was vitally aware of Marcos's presence. Her tingling nerves told her that while *she* might be exerting self-control, he had imposed no such ban on himself. Nor could she repress her thoughts.

Those few days in Athens when she'd had Marcos's exclusive attentions had spoiled her. The restrictive presence of his relations irked her. She wanted to be alone with Marcos again, and she wanted him to finish that interrupted sentence. What *had* he been meaning to ask her?

At a sign from the religious aunt, the ladies rose and left the table, adjourning to a nearby salon, furnished with all the elegance of a land-based drawing-room.

Chryssanti made no secret of the fact that she disliked this formal arrangement. Her mind was not on the conversation of her female relatives. Instead her eyes were constantly straying to the door through which Christos must eventually emerge.

Lena, with the control of her greater maturity, was better able to conceal her own eagerness for the men to rejoin them. But she feared her manner must be almost as *distraite*.

Fortunately the Mavroleons were engrossed in their family reunion, some of them Lena gathered, not having seen each other since the last similar occasion. When the men finally left the dining salon, conversation became general but none the less reminiscent. Their forthcoming visit to Thalassios Mavroleon, now the most senior member of the family, seemed to have evoked a mood of nostalgia for the past.

Lena was aware of Chryssanti's restlessness. But for herself she was fascinated by the fond anecdotes of their native islands. Proudly they named the hardy, austere, thrifty old seadogs who had laid the foundations of their family fortunes. And, more recent family history, that of Thalassios Mavroleon himself and his stolid, stubborn maintenance of fortune and tradition. Greek shipowners were no longer the hardy, intrepid captains of yore. But even in their silk suits on this luxury yacht they kept the spirit of their ancestors alive.

A surreptitious glance at her watch told Lena it was long past Stephen's normal bedtime. With an explanatory word to Anastasia, she shepherded him to the cabin he was sharing with Manoli Mavroleon. It was impossible to rush a small boy's bedtime, and she was absent for some while. When she returned to the salon it was to find most of the company had dispersed, the older aunts and uncles presumably to their beds. Only a few die-hards were left quietly chatting and sipping their drinks. None of the younger generation was left.

Lena had hoped for some conversation with Marcos, and it was with a sense of disappointment that, unnoticed, she left the salon once more. She made her way to her own suite, expecting to find Chryssanti there. But there was no sign of the younger girl. With a sigh she supposed she must go in search of her. Her responsibility for Chryssanti did not end until the girl was safely in her grandfather's home and accepted by him. But where on earth, on a vessel this size, did she begin her search?

It was dark now, and the *Poseidon*'s rigging lights were strung like diamonds against the night sky. The sea was still but for the moving lights of late-homing fishing-boats. In the distance were the twinkling lights of shore, and from somewhere drifted the faint sound of *bou-zouki* music. Serene moonlight gave enough illumination for Lena to see that the for'ard deck was deserted. She made her way aft, to the pool deck.

The floodlit pool might have been in someone's back garden instead of on board a yacht. Surrounding it were tubs and urns containing flowering plants and shrubs. Someone was swimming, covering its length from end to end in long, powerful overarm strokes. It didn't take Lena long to realise that it was Marcos. She hesitated, knowing she ought to go on with her search for Chryssanti, yet wanting to watch him a little longer, unobserved.

But, as she hesitated, he surfaced suddenly and saw her. He didn't say anything but trod water, making his way slowly to the edge of the pool. His eyes never left hers and Lena found herself rooted to the spot, aware of an idiotic impulse to run. But some stronger urge held her.

Fascinated, she watched as the water receded from his gleaming, olive-skinned body, leaving its dark hairs sleek and flat. She'd never seen him without clothing of some kind, and had never realised before quite how muscu-larly perfect he was, his body sculptural in its per-fection, like those of the marble gods his ancestors had venerated.

She realised that her legs were trembling, her mouth dry, and somewhere within her an insidious aching had begun, the need to be held to such a hard, perfect body. Her fingertips tingled with the urge to glide over that smooth, damp flesh and explore its contours. Nervously, she licked her lips, and at last he spoke.

'Why don't you come in?'

'I . . . I'm hardly dressed for it.' She tried for lightness, but the words came out in a rusty croak.

'No problem. We always have costumes for guests. I'm sure we have one to fit you. Go and take a look.' He gestured towards the side of the pool, towards a row of changing-rooms.

'No, I . . . it's a bit late for swimming. Perhaps tomorrow.'

'Tomorrow the pool will be full. Tonight we have it to ourselves.' What an inducement! Yet still she shook her head.

'I ought to find Chryssanti. She's not in the cabin.'

'She's quite safe. Christos and his brothers are looking after her. They're in the games room, playing table tennis. Relax, Lena,' he coaxed, 'you're off duty. Make the most of it.'

Why not? This was what she'd been wanting all evening, to be alone with him. And what more perfect setting?

'All right.' With a sudden decisive nod, she moved towards the poolside cabins.

As Marcos had suggested, there were costumes in plenty. Some of them were new and obviously unworn. They certainly hadn't been purchased with his aunts in mind, Lena thought, somewhat dismayed by their brevity. Finally she close a black two-piece, admitting wryly to herself that she had chosen it because it was the most flattering to her golden-tanned body and sun-lightened blonde hair. Nevertheless, it was with a feeling of painful self-consciousness that she returned to the pool and found herself subjected to Marcos's critical appraisal.

She had hoped to slip into the pool unnoticed, but he was sitting on the edge waiting for her, and his black eyes travelled the length of her before he spoke.

'A veritable water-nymph. The sea gods will envy me tonight.' He certainly had a good line in compliments, she thought wryly. Was it just a line, or was he sincere? She wished she knew.

'I'm afraid I don't swim very well,' she confessed.

'Then you must practise regularly while you have the opportunity. Come,' he held out his hand, 'let me see you. Perhaps I can help you to improve.'

She slid into the water. It was invitingly, silkily warm, like the skin of the man who now supported her.

'Please,' she said with a breathlessness not caused by her immersion, 'I can manage. I'm not *that* bad. I won't drown.' Yet, contrarily, it was a disappointment when he released her.

Lena had only ever learned breast-stroke, though she had often admired and envied those who could manage the more powerful crawl. But in her busy life swimming had taken a low priority. She swam a length then surfaced. Holding on to the side, she looked around for Marcos and found him close beside her.

'As you say, you are not too bad,' he commented. 'But the arm and leg movements could be improved. Let me show you.' He pulled her down into the water again, and a bemused Lena found herself floating on her front, one of his hands supporting her stomach while with the other he moved first her arm and then a leg in demonstration.

She hoped he would think it was the movement of the water and not her reactions to him that made her quiver so.

He freed her again and she did another length, trying to incorporate his instructions into her style. But it was difficult to concentrate, wondering if he would stop and hold her again. He did so.

'Stand here, in the shallower water. Face me. Give me your hands. Now this is how you should move your arms, so!'

As her arms moved Lena lost her footing on the smooth marble tiles of the pool and, water-borne, glissaded forward, colliding with a hard, muscular chest.

She floundered to regain her feet, and the success of her struggles brought the entire length of her body into contact with his. At the impact, automatically his arms closed about her, steadying her. She raised her head to apologise and met his eyes.

It was impossible to drown in four feet of water, she thought dizzily, but it was quite possible to drown in the depths of this man's brilliant black eyes as they held hers in a long-drawn-out gaze. Her hands had come to rest on his chest, and beneath her palms she could feel the steady thump of his heart. Had its beat accelerated as she knew hers had done? She didn't know, but she felt his ribcage lift and fall in a long breath, and there was a certain rigidity in his thighs, pressed against hers, that made her suspect he was not unmoved by their proximity.

CHAPTER FOUR

THE touch of that stunningly virile body was playing havoc with *her* senses. Marcos continued to look into her eyes for a moment, then, gently but firmly, he put her away from him.

'I think perhaps that is enough instruction for to-night,' he said.

'Y—yes, of course,' she stammered. 'Thank you.'

Blindly she reached for the edge of the pool. It must be the chlorinated water that was making her eyes smart. Thank God Marcos hadn't been able to read her thoughts just then, when she could have sworn he was about to kiss him. And she would have let him, would have returned his kisses eagerly.

'Helena!'

'Yes?' Standing on the side, she dared not turn to look at him.

'We were interrupted earlier.' Now she did turn, slowly tremulously. 'I was going to ask you something.'

'Yes.' Her heart was beating an uneven tattoo against her ribcage.

'What do you plan to do, *after* you have handed over Irini's children on Skiapelos?'

'Do?' she said flatly. 'I don't understand.'

'Will you be returning to England?' He swung himself out of the water to stand beside her, his brief black trunks were moulded closely to his body, leaving very little to her already fevered imagination.

'Not . . . not immediately,' she said, low-voiced.

'What then?'

'I'd planned to travel a bit more.'

'You have no job to return to?'

'I handed in my notice just before I left England.'

'That was rash, *ne*? I understand jobs are hard to come by these days.'

'I don't expect any trouble. I'm well qualified. Besides, I might decide to work abroad for a while.'

'What *are* your qualifications?'

'I have a degree in business studies. I...I was a PA in a large firm in London.' She prayed he wouldn't press for more details.

'Hmm.' He picked up a large towel from a poolside chair and wrapped it around her shoulders, his touch sending shafts of agonising sensation through her. 'Remind me again, nearer the time. I may be able to help.'

To work for Marcos? To see him perhaps every day, but to know that he was out of her reach? It could only be a cause of grief.

'I don't know that I'll want to stay in Greece.'

'You do not like my country?' He sounded amazed.

'You *know* I do!' Then, less vehemently, 'But it's not the only country in the world.'

'You wish to see the world before you settle down.' He nodded understandingly. 'But you *do* intend to stay in one place some day, to marry, perhaps?'

She drew in a sharp, painful breath. 'I don't know. I thought so once. Now I'm not at all certain of my future.'

'There is perhaps a possibility of reconciliation with...?'

'No!' It was unthinkable.

'You sound very positive.'

She was. Lena knew with a deep certainty that, if Petros were to come to her tomorrow and beg her to take him back, she would refuse. She *had* been in love with him, or so she'd thought. But that had been a poor emotion compared with that she now felt for Marcos Mavroleon. She'd known Petros for almost two years. But, incredibly, in that length of time her feelings for him had not deepened to the extent that, after just days she now felt for Marcos. Without any encouragement on his part, she was crazily, hopelessly in love with him. Her own apparent changeability worried her. She didn't like the idea that she might be fickle.

'I must go.' She had to get away on her own, to examine this revelation, to come to terms with it. But above all to convince herself of its uselessness. 'I must see that Chrys gets to bed at a reasonable time.'

'You are very conscientious.' He rested a hand on her shoulder, steering her towards the changing-rooms. Every nerve in her body screamed for him to take her in his arms, but it was only a casual, friendly gesture that anyone might make, she reminded herself. 'Goodnight, Helena. Sleep well.' Then, with apparent inconsequentiality, 'We have many more days ahead of us.'

Lena was thankful that Chryssanti was asleep when she finally reached the cabin they shared. She couldn't have borne to listen to any eulogies about Christos, when she must repress her own thoughts about his cousin. She wished she could fall so easily into restful slumber, but mind and body kept her awake for many hours, and next morning, heavy-eyed, she was awoken far too early by an enthusiastic Chryssanti. The younger girl was eager for a new day to start.

'I said I'd meet Christos and the others at the pool before breakfast,' she explained. Then, with a pout, 'I could do without Dimitri and Manoli, but they're very pushy.'

Despite her heart and body's urging to the contrary, Lena followed the advice of her head and avoided being alone with Marcos in the days that followed. She used the pool when the others did and avoided being up on deck at night. Tassia Mavroleon made her approval known.

'I see you are taking my advice, Helena. Believe me, it is for the best.'

The sixth day of their cruise brought them to their destination.

Lena was on deck with Stephen. Chryssanti was off somewhere about her own pursuits, with Christos no doubt. Stephen was a well-behaved child. His play required only a token supervision, and Lena was gazing wistfully out to sea, her thoughts far away, when she saw land rising on the horizon.

'Those are the islands of Skiapelos, Helena.' Marcos had caught her, for once, unaware of his presence. He came to stand beside her at the rail. 'The main island, which is my grandfather's home, and five subsidiary islands. Another half-hour and we shall be there.'

'I'd better find Chrys.' She turned to leave. 'Stephen, come...'

'Wait!' Marcos's hand on her arm detained her. 'There is plenty of time for that. I would like you to watch with me. It is a sight not to be missed.' There was an edge of eager anticipation to his voice.

'Then surely Chrys should be...'

'Helena, are you trying to avoid me?' His eyes were no longer on the horizon, but on her face in curious scrutiny. 'I have seen nothing of you alone these past few days. Have I offended you in some way?'

'N... no, of course not. How could you?'

'That is what I am asking myself. I cannot recall...'

'You've done nothing, Marcos, honestly. I...'

'Then prove it by staying with me, hmm?'

What could she say, or do? She leant once more against the rail, needing its support to offset the weakness she felt at his nearness. He leant companionably beside her, his arm, his shoulder, his thigh touching hers. In exquisite anguish, Lena clenched her teeth and stared ahead.

As the yacht moved ever closer to land, she began to pick out details of the sloping green rock that was the main island. It was picturesque to the point of drama: a tightly enclosed blue harbour full of brightly painted fishing caiques, and above it a little town of squat, whitewashed cubist buildings stained tangerine in the sunlight, with steep hills beyond.

The yacht's steady engines ceased, the anchor chain rattled and they were stationary. The launch was lowered and there was a sudden bustle and movement of people. Again Marcos's hand on her arm stayed Lena.

'Let the aunts and uncles go first. They will be eager to greet their brother.' He looked down at her. 'I do not want you to be nervous, Helena.'

'Nervous? Of what?' Nothing could be more nerve-racking, she thought, than being close to this man, wanting him with a ferocity of desire of which she hadn't known herself capable.

'Of meeting my grandfather. He is not a monster.'

'Just a tyrant,' she riposted.

'A tyrant, maybe,' he agreed, 'but a loving tyrant, as you will see.'

As Marcos would be some day, she knew with a sudden certainty, snatching a sideways glance at the profile which, though not exactly handsome, was now to her the most attractive, the most compelling she had ever seen. She could picture him as the patriarch of Skiapelos, in his grandfather's place, with a wife, family, relations gathering to pay him tribute. Already he had a quality of leadership that others recognised. Christos and his brothers deferred to Marcos's every edict. But if he was going to follow in his grandfather's footsteps he was leaving it a little late to found his own dynasty. He must be around thirty-five. Before she could prevent it, the question popped out.

'Why have *you* never married, Marcos?' The answer was as disconcerting as her own temerity.

'I have been waiting for my bride to grow up.' Her face must have reflected her shock, for he went on, 'You are probably not familiar with our marriage customs?'

'I know about arranged marriages,' Lena said, the words coming with painful slowness. 'Your aunt Irini... But I thought maybe attitudes had relaxed a little since then.' The Theodopoulos family hadn't objected to her engagement to Petros.

'In mainland Greece, perhaps. Many island families prefer the old ways. I was betrothed at seventeen.'

'You obviously believe in tradition, then?'

'In some of them,' he agreed.

The launch was returning and there was no time for further questions and answers. Which was probably just as well, if she were to cover up her stunned reaction to his revelation. Idiotic of her, of course, to have imagined there was no woman in Marcos's life.

But Marcos seemed blithely unaware of her mental withdrawal. He continued to talk as they made their way to the launch and during the short journey ashore.

'Marianthe Lychnos is the great-grandaughter of my grandfather's oldest friend. When she was born, it was agreed that she should be betrothed to me, and on her eighteenth birthday we should be married.'

'H . . . how old is she now?' She had to know.

'In three months' time she will be eighteen.'

'Does . . . does *she* live on Skiapelos?'

'No. She comes from Mykonos, but she will be at my grandfather's name day celebrations. You will like her.'

Lena wasn't so sure, and as Marcos handed her into the launch she was too *distraite* even to register the usual throb of her pulses at his touch. In three months Marcos would be married, and very shortly she would have to endure seeing him with his fiancée. Fool, she told herself irritably, you should have stuck to your resolution and steered clear of men for a while. Talk about out of the frying pan into the fire.

The main island of Skiapelos had its own harbour flanked by long white pebble beaches. Lena wasn't quite sure what she'd expected. Certainly not this thriving community of flat-roofed asymmetrical white houses, so crowded together that they grew out of one another like fungi on a tree bole, and streets with a tiny blue-domed church on nearly every corner. It was true the cobbled streets seemed fit only for dwarfs or for the donkeys that carried them up the hill from the seafront. Thank heaven she'd worn trousers this morning.

The heavy, oppressive air was filled with the varying scents of flowers, dung, the sea and cooking. As the twisting lanes tacked to and fro, every bend gave a new vista of harbour, town and surrounding hillsides.

Marcos edged his donkey alongside Lena's, his dignity not a whit impaired by the animal's low stature.

'What do you think of our island?'

'It's very attractive, but somehow I hadn't pictured your grandfather living in one of these little houses.'

Marcos's laugh was a deep, attractive sound that stirred her to unbearable depths.

'He was born in such a house, and for that reason this little town is carefully preserved. He lives very differently now—not perhaps from choice but from expediency. Wealth has its responsibilities.'

Lena soon saw what he meant. On the far side of the island the land sloped down more gently to the sea. There were no steep, precipitous pathways. Another much larger man-made harbour gave easier access to a made-up road which ran inland to a vast green area enclosed by white-painted ranch-style fencing. Within this enclosure sprawled a villa, blindingly white against the blue sky. As they drew nearer Lena could see the traditional blue outlines painted around doors and long windows that stood open to the sun on all sides. By the main door was parked a large limousine. And surely, she looked back towards the harbour again, that was the *Poseidon* gliding in to anchor. Puzzled, she turned to Marcos.

'Then why on earth anchor in the other harbour and go through all that performance with the donkeys?' But, with a wry expression, before he could answer, she groaned, 'No, don't tell me! It's tradition!'

He laughed in appreciation of her dry humour, his head thrown back, exposing the bronzed column of his neck.

'You must be thinking us a very odd family.' He sobered. 'But there *is* a very good reason. We Greeks have our pride, you know, and the villagers of Skiapelos, indebted as they are in many ways to my grandfather's bounty, like to feel they are offering a service in return—hence the donkey transport. Needless to say, there are times when the new harbour and my grandfather's heli-pad are used. Building materials and other heavy items could scarcely be brought up here on donkeyback. Neither could infirm visitors. And confess, Lena, you would have found it a very mundane proceeding to be whisked from yacht to villa by helicopter and limousine, missing the sights and sounds of island life?' He was right, of course.

The next few moments were filled with activity as a veritable army of servants, almost as many as there were guests, took over shepherding people to their rooms. Lena received a confused impression of white walls hung with Old Masters, of illumined niches which held sculptured treasures she longed to stop and examine. According to Marcos, she and Irini's children were not expected, and yet a suite of rooms was placed at their disposal. She could only assume that because the villa was so extensive there was always accommodation available, whatever the number of visitors arriving.

She had been expecting to share with Chryssanti, but instead there were separate rooms with a communicating sitting-room, and Stephen was whisked away to a separate nursery-room where, he was assured, there would be children of his own age.

Luggage had been brought up from the yacht, and Lena unpacked for herself and Chryssanti, then, at a loss to know what she was supposed to do next, she took stock of her surroundings. Her bedroom possessed a balcony with sweeping views of the sea below while the sitting-room overlooked a shady, vine-covered patio that separated one wing of the villa from another. In the centre of the patio, by a gently murmuring fountain, a pretty dark-haired girl sat reading and, as Lena ventured out on to the cool marble tiles, the girl looked up and gave a friendly smile. She closed her book and rose to her feet.

'Kalispera, thespinis!'

'Good afternoon,' Lena replied.

'Ah, you're English.' The girl slipped into that language, which she spoke with an easy colloquialism. 'Have you come with Marcos's party?' And, as Lena nodded, 'So he's here at last. Everyone will be gathering to greet Kyrios Thalassios. Shall we join them?'

Lena was glad of a guide to the villa's rambling corridors. She called Chryssanti, and together they made their way back to the main reception hall, a large area of tiled marble floors, the high ceiling supported by slim Doric columns. Here the other guests were assembling in noisy reunion.

'Heavens, what a crowd,' Lena exclaimed. There were even more people than those who had arrived on the *Poseidon*.

'Kyrios Mavroleon is a very respected man,' the girl explained. 'None of his friends or family would dream of missing his name day—the feast of *Aghios Thalassios*. Oh, there's Marcos. Excuse me.' She left Lena's side and hurried across the room to where Marcos stood in conversation with a group of other men, and Lena saw her put a hand on his arm.

Marcos glanced down and his face lit up into a welcoming smile. As his arm went around the girl's waist and he bent to kiss her cheek, Lena came to an inescapable conclusion. As Marcos straightened, his glance caught Lena's and she shuddered to think what emotions her face might be registering. He spoke a few swift words to the girl at his side, then drew her back to where Lena and Chryssanti stood.

'Helena, I gather you two have not introduced your-selves. This is Marianthe Lychnos.' Lena held out her hand. 'I have explained to Marianthe who you are, and about Chryssanti and Stephanos, and she has kindly of-fered to look after you during your stay here.' And with unconscious irony he added, 'I should like the two of you to be friends.'

Perhaps fortunately for Lena's lacerated feelings there was no opportunity to make a suitable reply, for at that moment there was a perceptible stir in the assembled crowd, followed by a silence that, considering the recent level of decibels, was uncanny. All eyes were upon the doorway which framed a solitary figure. This must be Thalassios Mavroleon.

He certainly had a theatrical sense of timing, Lena thought as he remained stationary for a long moment before advancing into the salon, a tall, rather beautiful old man with a Byronic profile, curling white hair and flashing dark eyes.

Then there were many cries of *'Chronia polla'*—'Many years', the traditional greeting on someone's name day, Marianthe told Lena.

The sense of protocol she had noticed aboard the yacht was observed here too, relations approaching him in strict order of seniority and rank. It was like a royal audience. It was amusing and yet it was awe-inspiring too, and this was the man she would have to face with her story of Irini and her errand here.

It was a long time before Marcos came towards her, took her by the hand and led her over to his grandfather.

'*Poppa*, may I present *Thespinis* Thomas, our visitor from England. Miss Thomas has a special errand here, which I hope you will allow her to tell you about during her stay.'

The flashing dark eyes under shaggy white brows regarded Lena sternly.

'*Thespinis*, I do not allow business affairs to interfere with family occasions.' His English was stilted perfection.

'This isn't business, Mr Mavroleon, I assure you.' For different reasons, Thalassios Mavroleon had much the same effect upon her nervous system as his grandson.

'Then I will grant you half an hour this evening, before the celebrations commence.' The white head nodded a dismissal.

'That,' Lena told Chryssanti wryly, as she returned to her place by the younger girl, 'was your grandfather. Wow!'

'He's very handsome,' Chryssanti said consideringly. 'Didn't he want to meet Stephen and me?'

'First,' Lena said with feeling, '*I* have to break it to him that you exist—that you're *here*!'

That promised half-hour came round a little too quickly for Lena, even though, in the past two weeks, she had rehearsed over and over again what she would say to Thalassios Mavroleon. It was a relief when it was Marcos who came to conduct her to the interview.

'I thought you might prefer me to be present?'

'Oh, yes, thank you!' Her gratitude was profound. 'Frankly, I'm terrified.'

'He will not bite you,' Marcos reassured.

'No,' Lena conceded, 'but he looks as if he might bark a lot.'

Marcos gave that familiar shout of laughter which so illuminated his normally serious features.

'I like this about you very much, Lena. Come.' Suddenly he took her hand. His touch was very warm and comforting, but equally it was disturbing. 'Let your

courage be as great as your sense of humour. My grandfather admires courage, as do I.'

Thalassios Mavroleon received them in his own suite
of rooms, in his study. Here there were no paintings,
but framed photographs of ships and horses. On his desk
was a bronzed sculpture of a racehorse which his long
fingers caressed constantly as they talked.

At first, at the mention of his daughter's name, the
handsome old face became closed and unresponsive, and
Lena feared the interview would be terminated before
she could conclude her prepared speech. But Thalassios
Mavroleon was a man of his word. He had promised
her half an hour and half an hour she should have.

'Does Irini imagine that I have forgotten her behaviour?' he demanded of Lena at one point. 'We Greeks
have long memories.'

'Not forgotten, perhaps,' Lena conceded pacifically,
'but I think she hopes you've found it in your heart to
forgive her.'

'Perhaps *you* can tell me, *thespinis*, why I *should*
forgive her?'

Remembering the white-faced Irini and guessing what
it had cost her in terms of pride to appeal to her father,
Lena knew a flash of impatience with the unbending,
implacable old man.

'She *is* your daughter!'

'I disowned her when she disobeyed me.'

'How about common humanity, then?' Lena's blue
eyes darkened, a sign that betokened anger to those who
knew her. 'Your daughter is probably going to die. I
know *I* couldn't live with *my* conscience if I let someone
die without my forgiveness, especially for something
so . . . so petty.'

It was Thalassios's turn to show anger. The black eyes, still young in the lined face and still as eloquent as his grandson's, flashed fire.

'You think our traditions, deference to family authority are *petty*? Believe me, *thespinis*, if your generation had more respect for such things, the world would be a better place.'

'Don't you think it would be a better place too,' Lena demanded, 'if *your* generation had a stronger spirit of forgiveness and compassion?'

'You are very outspoken, *thespinis*,' he said gruffly, with a lowering look under his shaggy brow, 'and, I remind you, you are a guest under my roof.'

'I'm sorry if I seem impertinent,' Lena said stiffly, 'but I feel very strongly about this. And if I've offended against your hospitality, I'll leave.'

The verbal battle had waged to and fro so vigorously, neither prepared to cede an inch, that Lena had quite forgotten Marcos's presence. It was a shock when he intervened.

'*Poppa*, Miss Thomas is only an emissary. She undertook this errand in good faith and feels a responsibility. She does not deserve the anger you feel towards Aunt Irini, nor do Irini's children, surely?'

There was an interminable silence. It was impossible to tell what thoughts or emotions went on in the head behind the elderly aristocratic face. But either Lena must have made a better advocate than she knew, or Marcos's intervention had done the trick, for at last Thalassios cleared his throat and pronounced, 'I will meet Irini's children, *thespinis*. Bring them to me tomorrow morning,' he commanded, 'early, before the celebrations recommence.'

* * *

When the Greeks celebrated, they really went to town, Lena thought much later that night. After a meal of many courses, some of which Lena had to refuse, there was music and dancing. The guests threw themselves into enjoyment and yet tradition was still evident, giving the riotousness a pattern and shapeliness.

'This is your chance to hear the old music,' Marcos told her. 'The music of our villages and islands, the music of *tsambouna*, *clarino* and *santouri*—bagpipes, clarinet and dulcimer,' he translated.

As the night wore on and the wine flowed freely, the Mavroleon family and their guests became more and more uninhibited. Those with good voices were called upon to get up and sing, a favourite song being taken up by the whole company. The energetic danced in frenetic solo performances, the younger, wilder element balancing wineglasses or bottles on their heads in an atmosphere of mounting *kephi*—good spirits. It was a whole world away from the sophisticated city parties of the Theodopouloses, but Lena found she was enjoying it hugely so long as no one expected such exhibitionism from *her*.

She could not understand the words of the songs with their long, agonised and questioning notes, but somehow Marcos always seemed to be at hand to explain. The lyrics seemed to deal mostly with the ups and downs of love—'Will you not tell me if you love me? Or with a kiss, drive away my pain?' She found the words, murmured in her ear by his husky voice, infinitely disturbing. If only he were saying them to her, instead of just translating.

In the small hours of the morning, the hardier souls who remained danced in groups, and Lena did find herself drawn into a performance of the *stae tria*, a circle dance in which the circle was never complete, but was led by a dancer who supplied special effects of leaps, foot slaps and kicks which caused much hilarity as his followers tried to emulate them. Flushed and laughing, she was aware more than once of Marcos's eyes on her.

Mercifully, around dawn the musicians slowed to a throbbing, ambulatory pace. Lena was sought by many partners, and at last she found herself dancing with Marcos, a situation she had dreamed of but never hoped to realise. An inner voice warned her that it was madness to allow herself to feel this way as they swayed around the floor, her body close to his, the warmth and the masculine scent of him drugging her senses, forming images for the memory to hold thereafter. Tired, yet unwilling for the night to end, she moved in a dreamlike state of euphoria in which anything was possible.

For the evening's events she had chosen to wear a cocktail-length, backless dress and suddenly she became aware of Marcos's fingers tracing her spine. It was an exquisite torment which set her body on fire for more. After a while he pulled her closer, and she was startled to find him fully aroused. It must be the wine and the music having their effect. She tried to ease herself away from him, but as she did so his clasp tightened, restraining her, and it seemed to her that he deliberately moulded her body to his in a way he hadn't been doing before. She ought to protest, to make more of an effort to escape the intimacy of his embrace, yet she didn't want him to stop what he was doing to her.

'Are you enjoying yourself, Helena?' he asked, his voice a husky murmur against her temple.

'Oh, yes,' she said fervently, then flushed hotly in case he misunderstood. 'I mean . . . it's been a lovely evening. It's always a pity when something has to come to an end,' she gabbled, sinkingly aware of compounding her gaffe and of his amusement.

'It need not end just yet,' he told her, 'if that is what you wish for. You have seen a Greek sunset. Let me show you the sunrise.'

'Oh, but . . .' she faltered. 'I don't think . . . Marianthe might not . . . I mean . . .'

'Marianthe went to bed long ago.'

'That's not the point. I . . .'

'And I assure you she will have no objection. Why should she?' His question seemed to imply that Lena was assuming more than he offered. Of course, why *shouldn't* he show a guest one of the attractions of his home? That *was* all he was offering, and by demurring she was making it sound as if she suspected his motives.

'In that case . . .'

Beyond the cultivated and tended grounds of the villa, a little gate opened into a grove of crooked olive trees dark with shadows. Lena was not sure she would have wanted to come here alone. Highly imaginative, she found it almost possible to believe in the mischievous satyrs of the ancient Greeks, lurking behind the gnarled trees, spying on them with lascivious eyes, able to read her thoughts.

As they walked, gradually the tips of the leaves began to lighten, and when they emerged on to the far side of the grove the sun began to rise. Slowly at first, the grey veil of night receded before the dawn, with the promise of light in the mysterious pinkish glow that deepened and grew. At last, above the neighbouring islands the sun showed itself with a dazzle of gold that sparked a pattern of burnished ripples across the waters of the bay beneath. With the coming of the sun, colour drenched back into the landscape.

'Well, was it worth it?' Marcos asked. As they watched he had draped a casual arm about her shoulders, his nearness adding to the intensity of an experience she thought she would never forget.

'Oh, yes,' Lena breathed.

They were in a place of wild grass, bleached blonde as honey, where worn lichened steps led to a hollow place of fallen marble stones.

'It is an old garden,' Marcos told her. 'Heaven knows how long it has been here. Probably the private temple of some ancient Greek, destroyed by an earthquake centuries ago. My grandfather calls it "The Garden of the Gods" and insists that it remain just as it is.'

Surely they should be turning back now? But with his arm still about her he led her further into the wilderness of mossy marble—an enchanted place that owed its enchantment to his presence, to the fugitive brush of his thigh against hers.

'The Garden of the Gods,' Marcos said again, but musingly this time. 'Probably the gods were no more than larger-than-life human beings conjured up by the imagination of a simple people. Their loves, and their lusts too, were probably just a magnified version of the normal tendencies in men and women.' As he looked down at her, his back was to the now blinding sunlight so that his face was in shadow, hers exposed to its full glare. With an unexpectedness that gave her no time for evasion, he took her face in his hands. 'You laughed at me when I compared you to Helen of Troy. But yours *is* a face that might drive a mortal, let alone a god, to do many things.'

Lena moved uneasily as an inner fire coiled and twisted in an unbearable, burning ache. She swallowed.

'Marcos, I...'

'No, let me finish. Let me look at you. Your eyes make the Aegean pale by comparison, and when you look at me as you are looking now, I feel I am drowning in their depths.' He had a poetic turn of phrase enhanced by his slightly accented, throaty voice. He went on with his verbal seduction. 'You have a delicate bone-structure that will still be beautiful when you are old. And your mouth...' At last his fertile imagery seemed to have run out. Instead he bent and brushed his lips across hers. 'I have wanted to do that for a very long time.'

'Marcos, you shouldn't...'

'Why not?' he challenged. 'For the moment let us forget everything except that here we are a god and goddess to whom everything is possible.' As though in agreement, the leaves of the olive trees rustled in a sudden delicate shiver of wind, as though something or someone living but invisible gave agreement to his words.

His hands took a strong grip of her shoulders, holding her as though she might try to run away. He was going to kiss her again, she knew, and yet tantalisingly he was taking his time about it, studying her face again as though he would memorise it feature by feature. Then he moved a pace or two, taking her with him; leaning against a tree, he pulled her to him. With one arm he held her tightly, while his free hand stroked her throat. Quiver after quiver shook Lena's body, and weak with sensation she closed her eyes in a blankness of mindless enjoyment. Resisting, protesting no longer, mutely she awaited his pleasure.

'*Kalliste!* Most beautiful!' he murmured as his fingers continued to play over her neck and shoulders, exploring and shaping the delicate bones he had admired. Strangely, the delicacy of his touch, the tantalising slowness of his caresses, were as excitingly sensuous as greater ardour from another man might have been. He was driving her wild with a need to know more, much more. But as yet he seemed content. He seemed to make no demand of her that she should touch him in return, and without his implicit invitation she felt shy of doing so.

But when his mouth closed over hers again with the passionate fierceness she had longed for, she could restrain herself no longer. The hands that had rested passively on his chest rose to clasp about his strong neck, and at the feel of crisp, virile hair beneath her fingers she shuddered convulsively, pressing herself to him, a betraying little murmur of need escaping her lips.

She felt the swift rise and fall of his chest as his arms tightened. He pressed her closer still, leaning further into the supporting tree, and she felt the fierce virility of him.

She arched her back in willing surrender. She seemed almost to have stopped breathing as his hands slid down her spine, cupped her buttocks and pressed her to him with a violence that betrayed the force of his own desire.

The kiss went on and on until Lena felt she must faint under the force of her own needs. Driven mad by the unslaked demands of her body, she no longer cared that Marcos belonged to someone else. She only knew that *she* wanted to belong to *him*, fully, here, now. She murmured imploringly in her throat and gradually his kiss gentled, until finally he lifted his head and held her a little away from him.

'Marcos?' she implored, but he gave his head a little shake, not merely as a negative, but as though he sought to clear it.

'No,' he told her huskily. 'I think that is enough—for now.'

CHAPTER FIVE

SHE gazed at him in bemusement, but at that instant she was not unhappy. His words, disappointing though they were, seemed to promise other occasions.

'How do you like the idea of a Greek wedding?' he said to her as they began to walk back towards the villa.

Lena started, and for a moment her foolish heart thudded expectantly, but sanity returned as he went on, 'Because you may have the opportunity to attend one while you are here.'

'I shan't be here *that* long,' she said immediately, and saw his eyebrows rise.

'Since the wedding takes place this week, and you can scarcely leave Skiapelos without me...'

Lena's stomach rose and plummeted sickeningly, and her tongue cleaved drily to the roof of her mouth.

'You said it wasn't for another three months,' she managed to croak, revealing very clearly where her thoughts lay.

For a moment he looked puzzled, then he smiled enigmatically.

'But I wasn't referring to *my* wedding.'

'You weren't?' Relief made her dizzy, but it was only a temporary reprieve for common sense had fully re-asserted itself now. Those moments in the grove could have meant very little to Marcos. She should never have allowed them to happen, she scolded herself. The rider to his words had been only a gentle let-down for the urgency he'd sensed in her. There would be no other occasions. *She* must see to that. Marcos was betrothed to Marianthe Lychnos.

She felt tired now, really tired, so that it was an effort to put one foot in front of another. And, as she had discovered long ago, when she was tired it was easy to give way to depression. Marcos seemed attuned to her change of mood.

'Bed for you, Helena. Today everyone will sleep until late.'

'*I* can't,' she reminded him. 'Your grandfather wants to see Chrys and Stephen this morning—early. And I'd better not be late. I'm in his bad books already.'

She managed to catch a couple of hours' sleep, however, despite her conviction that her unhappy thoughts would keep her awake. But she woke feeling unrefreshed and filled with pessimism, not so much over the coming encounter with Thalassios, but regarding her life in general. She didn't seem to be very lucky in love. One man had jilted her, the next wasn't free to return her love.

'*You* don't look like a Mavroleon!' Thalassios told Chryssanti bluntly. 'No one in our family ever had red hair.' His attention had been given first of all to Stephen, and he had grunted his approval of the small boy, who in looks at least reflected his Greek heritage.

'I'm *not* a Mavroleon!' Chryssanti retorted immediately. 'I'm a Forster—and I *like* having red hair.'

Lena confidently expected the heavens to descend in the form of Thalassios's wrath. Instead, unpredictably, he gave a crack of laughter that reminded her of his grandson.

'So you've got spirit, heh? You take after your mother in that, at least. Well, sit down, sit down,' he said impatiently, 'and tell me about yourself. Do you speak

Greek? *Thespinis*,' he gestured to Lena, 'you may go, if you wish.'

She did wish. Obviously she was still out of favour with the old autocrat of Skiapelos. Besides, tired and dispirited, she was having difficulty hiding her depression. But, she thought, a little indignantly, for the length of time she'd spent in his presence, Thalassios might as well have ordered one of his servants to bring the children to him, and *she* could have slept longer. Perhaps then she might have been able to see things in better proportion.

But at least the interview between Thalassios and his grandchildren was a successful one.

'He's gruff and he's bossy. He obviously thinks boys are more important than girls,' Chryssanti reported when she rejoined Lena, 'but I quite like him.'

It was a relief to Lena not to have to cope with a teenage rebellion, and yet it meant, in effect, that her task here was over. There was no reason now why she should not move on and do the rest of her sightseeing as she'd planned. But the thought brought no euphoria in its wake. There were still so many places she'd always wanted to visit, and yet somehow the thought of exploring them alone had lost its appeal. Seeing Athens and its environs with Marcos had spoiled her.

Well, you can't have Marcos for a guide, she told herself firmly. Face it, you can't *have* Marcos—for anything, she added with gloomy humour.

'Is there really no other way of getting back to the mainland?' she asked him when he came in search of her, wanting to know how the encounter between Thalassios and his grandchildren had gone. Her tone betrayed a little of her desperation.

'Are you tired of us already, then?' he reproached. It was not said jestingly, but as if her answer really mattered.

'N—no, of course not.' She could never tire of Marcos's company. 'But I'm not needed here any more. I've no further reason to impose on your grandfather's hospitality and...' She gestured helplessly.

'And you wish to get on with your own life,' Marcos finished for her.

'Y—yes, I suppose so.'

'Are you not certain?'

Of course she wasn't certain. She wasn't certain of anything except that she loved him and that, when he was anywhere near her, her body ached to know his.

'I really ought to look for work,' she explained.

'I promised to help you,' Marcos reminded her, then, coaxingly, 'Come, remain here as *my* guest for a few more days, hmm? When we return to Athens, you shall work.'

'For...for you?' she asked doubtfully. She didn't think that was wise, and he too looked uncertain. But for different reasons, it transpired.

'I am not sure that you would be qualified to work for me personally. We shall see,' he promised her with a wide, white smile, and it seemed she had agreed to stay. 'In my country,' Marcos told her with mock severity, 'women do not argue.'

Though her feelings for Marcos were futile, Lena still found it impossible to contain her curiosity about him. It was unwise, but it seemed she must know as much about him as possible, information to carry away with her when she finally left Greece.

'Don't you have a house of your own?' she asked him as they lounged beside the villa's pool one morning. 'Or do you look on this as your home?'

'This villa will be mine some day—after my grandfather's death—may it be long postponed!' He crossed himself as he spoke. Lena had noticed that the Mavroleons were intensely religious. On the donkey ride up from the harbour, they had crossed themselves as they passed every one of the small blue-domed churches. 'I have the house in Athens, of course. But I *do* have a place on Skiapelos that is exclusively mine. Would you like to see it? Now?'

'Oh, I . . .' she demurred. But he was on his feet.

'Come on! Yes, just as you are. You don't need clothes where we're going.'

A beaming chauffeur seemed to find nothing strange in running them down to the man-made harbour, clad only in their swimsuits.

At first Lena thought they were going out to the yacht, and the idea of being alone there with Marcos filled her with quivering alarm. Of course, some of the crew would be on board . . . But it was to a small caique that he led her. He sprang aboard the broad-bottomed craft, offered her his hand, and to her surprise set sail unaided.

'My ancestors founded their fortune with little boats like these,' he told her, when she commented on his seamanship. 'They carried their own wool and cheese to other islands and to the mainlands. Those little caiques, in time, grew into millions of tons of tankers and bulk carriers.' There was no doubt he was proud of his ancestry. He was as much of a traditionalist as his grandfather, Lena decided. The thought gave her no comfort. Marcos would never set aside Thalassios's plans for him.

'There is something extraordinarily satisfying about sailing a caique,' Marcos went on. 'A Greek loves his boat as he loves his woman.' A gesture of his hand encompassed the boat's lines, sturdy, amply curved and broad in the beam. If that was the comparison he was making, Lena thought wryly, her own slender lines could not appeal to him.

'There is a sense of triumph, as they shudder on the crest of a big wave, that is like the moment before a man's consummation with a woman.' His words were sensual, his voice husky and his eyes on Lena's face seemed to convey a message she had no right to read there. She swallowed convulsively.

'Where are we going?' she asked in an attempt to divert not only his thoughts but her own.

'I told you Skiapelos is made up of several islands?' She nodded. 'One of the smaller islands is mine. It was my father's before me—as my grandfather's eldest son.'

'Does it have a name?'

Marcos shrugged.

'It has never seemed necessary to name it. How would *you* like to choose a name for my island, Helena?'

'I wouldn't be so presumptuous,' she said quickly. 'It's got nothing to do with me.'

Marcos's island looked a wild little rock. It was in fact uninhabited, he told her.

'It is so small, it is not even shown on the maps. My father did not live long enough to do anything constructive with it. I may build here some day, or I may just keep it in its natural form—as a retreat.'

'Do you come here often, then?' Lena asked as Marcos handed her on to a white, sandy beach.

'When I have something I want to think over—a personal problem.'

It was difficult to imagine Marcos Mavroleon worrying about anything. She told him so and he smiled.

'No? Not even though you have yourself experienced an interview with my grandfather? Believe me, that can constitute a problem.'

'You're not *afraid* of him?' The autocratic Thalassios *was* intimidating, certainly. But somehow she couldn't picture Marcos being in awe of him. Marcos was too like his grandfather.

'Not afraid, no. But I respect him and I do not like having to displease him.'

'Does he "interview" you often, then?'

'Regularly, about the way I am running his company. Occasionally on personal family matters. But soon *I* must seek an interview with *him*.'

'And that's worrying you?'

'It requires careful thought, certainly.'

As they spoke Marcos had not released her hand, and he led her up the sloping beach and into the broom-covered hillocks beyond. In the warmth of the sun the golden tangle emitted a heavy, musky scent that mingled with that of brine and the warm, masculine odour of the man who strode beside her. Marcos never moved slowly, even in the most enervating heat, and Lena was breathless by the time they reached the island's core.

'It's very overgrown,' she ventured. 'Are there... are there likely to be snakes or anything?'

'One or two, maybe,' he conceded but, at her look of alarm, reassured her, 'but they aren't the poisonous kind.' Even so, she couldn't restrain a shudder. 'Relax, Helena——' his hand tightened on hers '—you are safe with me.'

She wasn't so sure about that. They were very much alone here. Even more alone than they would have been on the yacht, where at least the crew would have been within hailing distance.

A short climb and they reached the highest point of the island, which consisted of a fairly large plateau with a breathtaking all-round view of the sea and the other islands in the group. The clarity of the air was laden with the ambrosial scent of herbs.

'I have sometimes thought of building a house here,' Marcos confessed. 'Not a very large one—just big enough for myself and one other person.'

'Perhaps when you're married?' She probed the wound and found it still hurt. More than ever, in fact.

He didn't rise to the bait, instead suggesting, 'Let me show you the beach on the far side. There are caves where I used to play as a boy.' He would probably bring his own children here some day. Lena's heart contracted at the thought of children with Marcos's dark hair and olive features, his liquid black eyes. How she wished *she* could be the one to bear those children.

The caves were beautiful, much larger than she'd expected, hung with stalactites that hovered, their icy fingertips striving to reach those of the stalagmites below. It was beautiful, but it was cold. Lena commented on it.

'I never expected to feel cold in Greece.'

At once he was concerned and, with an arm about her, he led her once more on to the sunlit beach. It seemed sensible to follow his suggestion and lie on the soft white sand, allowing the sun to warm her chilled body. Marcos sat beside her, and covertly she studied his by now familiar profile. He was gazing out to sea and yet she had an idea his dark eyes were not registering the blue waters or the wheeling seabirds. Perhaps he was brooding on the interview with his grandfather, and she wondered idly what would be the subject under discussion.

She was warmer now, and she realised they had been on the island for a long time.

'Marcos?'

He turned to look at her, his eyes refocusing, and something in their expression troubled her.

'Sh—shouldn't we be getting back?'

'Not yet.'

She wished she hadn't disturbed his train of thought when he rolled over on to his stomach and lay close beside her, elbows planted in the sand, his hands supporting his head as he continued his intent observation of her.

Her body began to feel a heat that had nothing to do with the sun, and she moved restlessly.

'Is...is it safe to swim here?' she asked for the sake of something to say.

Again her words became a matter for regret as he stretched out a hand and entwined his fingers in her honey-coloured hair.

'You would like some more swimming lessons, hmm?'

She remembered how her last lesson had ended, and she flushed becomingly.

'Oh, no! No, I didn't mean...I just thought it would be nice to swim in the sea.'

'Why not?' He rose with suspicious alacrity and reached down to pull her up. Without releasing her hand, he began to run towards the sea, and a moment later they plunged into its warm, silky embrace.

Lena revelled in its gentle buoyancy, floating on her back as Marcos performed an energetic crawl. But he was soon back beside her, treading water. His eyes slid the length of her prone body, taking in the gentle swell of her breasts, emphasised by her swimsuit's brief cut.

Embarrassed, she shot upright in the water, then found she could not touch bottom. Marcos reached for her, supporting her. But suddenly it was not support he offered, his hands at her waist, moulding her against him.

'Helena!' Her name was a sudden urgent whisper, and his lips claimed hers as they parted in futile protest. It was a gentle kiss as his lips explored the inner softness of hers. She could not help her response and the kiss intensified, his hands sliding upwards. With dismay, she felt him unfasten the bikini top.

'Marcos, no!' she gasped as he began to caress her breasts, his dark head bent in fascinated attention to his own actions.

'Helena, yes!' he mocked gently. Then, more throatily, 'I told you the sea gods would be envious of me. And I plan to make them more envious yet.'

Senses heightened by his words and by his touch, she felt pulsating desire swamping her body in an insistent tide. His hands moved downwards as he kissed her throat, then the twin peaks of her breasts, and his fingers gently probed the waistband of the bikini bottom.

She reached for him, her fingers curling in his hair, and he continued his sensual torment, licking first one salty nipple, then the other. She could feel the taut, throbbing pressure of his thighs against hers, making her ache for appeasement.

She pressed her lips to his neck, delicately tasting the male texture of his skin, and with a muttered *'Christos'* he swung her up into his arms and began to wade for the shore, his mouth clamped firmly to hers. He set her on the warm strand and came down above her, his body blotting out the light that was no fiercer than that in his black eyes.

Then his warm, urgent mouth claimed hers again. She could feel and hear the ragged, uneven rasping of his breath.

'I want you, Helena,' he breathed.

'Oh, Marcos!' She said his name tremulously. Her own voice was unrecognisable, soft and husky with her need. She parted her lips for him and felt his tongue surge into her mouth, duelling sensuously with her own.

As the kiss went on she plunged deeper into a maelstrom of sensation: the erotic thrust of his tongue in her mouth, the tingling of her bare breasts under the caress of his hands, the feel of his hard maleness against her thigh.

Her hands glided over his warm, naked back, exploring its muscular breadth. His masculinity was overpowering, her need an urgent, primal one. She *wanted* him. She knew she had never wanted a man the way she wanted Marcos Mavroleon—and *he* wanted *her*.

And if she didn't do something about it right now they were going to give into that need! Shocked back into sanity, she wrenched herself free and scrambled shakily to her feet.

'No, Marcos! This is all wrong! For goodness' sake, you're engaged to Marianthe!'

He was slow to react, and when he stood up she saw that his arousal was not diminished by her violent rejection. Warily, she watched him, prepared for him to make a grab for her, and yet not knowing what she'd do if he did. He had her completely at his mercy, alone with him here on his island.

For a long time he held her gaze with his own.

'You're right!' he said harshly. Then, abruptly, he turned on his heel and plunged back into the sea.

Shakily, Lena sat down on a convenient rock. She was uncertain how she felt about his reaction. Relief warred with unhappy chagrin. It wasn't flattering to have him give up so easily.

When he returned, his olive-skinned body gleaming with water, he was in control once more.

'Time to go home,' he told her, as coolly as if nothing had occurred between them. Home! If only his home *were* hers.

The celebrations for Thalassios's name day carried on for the whole of the week. Greeks retired late and rose early, and Lena had never been so tired in her life, in spite of observing the traditional and very necessary afternoon siesta. Fair-skinned, she found the earth-cracking heat too much for her. By day the light was harsh and cruel. At night the floors, shutters and beams of the villa shifted, groaned and cracked in the warm air, disturbing her rest. She felt decidedly edgy, and at times quite bad-tempered.

Lena was not the only one apparently whose mood had been affected. On the last day of their stay on the island they were all to attend the village wedding Marcos had spoken of. But an hour before they were due to leave the villa, Chryssanti burst into Lena's room, her face, which in any case had the pallor of the true redhead, was white and strained. She had scarcely shut the door behind her when she broke into noisy, angry sobs, through which Lena could just discern the muffled words, 'He's a liar. I don't believe him. I *hate* him!'

It was some while before Lena could calm the girl sufficiently to enquire what was the matter.

'It's that Dimitri Mavroleon. He's a liar,' she repeated. 'He...he's always where he's not wanted.' By this, Lena presumed Chryssanti meant with herself and Christos. 'And now...now he's told me Christos is getting married when we get back to Athens. It can't be true, Lena. It can't. He's never even mentioned a girl-friend, Lena,' it was an agonised cry, 'I *love* him!'

It was ironic, Lena thought, as she tried to comfort the distraught girl. Here she was, murmuring platitudes such as 'time being a great healer'—'plenty of fish in the sea'. And all the time she knew the clichéd words convinced her as little as they convinced Chryssanti.

'I can't possibly go to this wedding,' Lena told Marcos. 'I...'

'But you are dressed for it.' His dark eyes admired her slender figure in the colourful cool cotton that clung tautly over her high, thrusting breasts and enhanced her slim waist and curving hips.

'I can't leave Chrys.'

'Is she not well?'

'She's unhappy about...about something, which is worse. There's no medicine I can give her for that.'

'She is worrying about her mother all of a sudden?' Taken up with her infatuation with Christos, Chryssanti had mentioned Irini rarely of late.

'No. Look, Marcos,' she felt a need to share the anxiety with someone else, 'she...she fancies herself in love with Christos, and Dimitri's just told her he's going to be married soon. Is Dimitri just mischief-making, or is it true?'

'Dimitri, a mischief-maker?' Marcos sounded astounded. 'Certainly not. He is quite correct.'

'Oh!' Lena was exasperated, her own troubles temporarily forgotten. 'I wish you'd *told* me. If Chryssanti had known sooner, she might have been spared this unhappiness.'

'I am sorry,' Marcos said sincerely. 'I must confess to having been too concerned with my own affairs. I did not notice what was happening.' He sounded annoyed with himself. 'It should have been my place, not Dimitri's, to issue a warning.'

'Oh!' Lena exclaimed again. 'You and your grandfather...all of you...you're all so...so *feudal*! I suppose your grandfather arranged Christos's wedding, too?' He nodded. 'Just as I thought. Thank heaven English people aren't hide-bound by all this tradition.' She remembered the reason she'd sought him out. 'Anyway, I'm not coming to the wedding.'

But she did go. Marcos would not take no for an answer.

'Marianthe will stay with Chryssanti. They are close in age.'

'But that would mean Marianthe missing the wedding,' Lena objected.

'Such events are no novelty to her. *You* are a visitor to our islands.'

And soon Marianthe would have her own wedding to look forward to, Lena reflected miserably.

Chryssanti didn't seem to care who stayed with her, or in fact if *anyone* did.

'I want to go home,' she told Lena between renewed sobs. 'I wish we'd never come here. I hate this place. I hate Greece, and most of all I *hate* Dimitri Mavroleon!'

'It's not his fault,' Lena tried to reason with her. Personally she liked Dimitri, who was about her own age—

a quieter, more introverted character than his younger brothers, Christos and Manoli.

She was glad she'd attended the wedding, even though the happiness of bride and groom and the traditional ceremony were a poignant reminder of Marcos's unattainability.

It took place in the old harbour village through which she'd passed on her arrival, and once again their transport was the patient donkeys. The wedding was an interesting and lovely spectacle. In one of the blue-domed churches bride and groom stood before the chanting white-robed and bearded priest. White crowns, bound together by a white ribbon, were placed on their heads, and the best man exchanged them back and forth. The newly-weds were then led around the altar three times, while the guests pelted them with fertility-bringing rice and flower petals. The ceremony over, every guest was given a *boboniera*—a small gift of sweetened almonds.

The marriage service was followed by a feast. Long tables had been set up in the streets down by the tiny harbour. Under the benevolent gaze of the priest, the guests consumed course after course, washed down with sweet white wine and finishing only as the sun dipped below the horizon. Then came the dancing—in the little village square, lit by flares and by moonlight. Many of the dancers were in costume, the women in full, colourful skirts banded with white, little pillbox hats and embroidered boleros. The men wore dark baggy trousers, wide cummerbunds and sleeveless jackets over full-sleeved white shirts. There was a touch of the Oriental in the plaintive music of violins, lutes and guitars.

'In the past,' Marcos told Lena, 'the celebrations would have gone on for five days.'

'You mean,' she said a trifle acidly, 'that you've actually done away with a *tradition*?' She felt a sudden desire to needle him, to vent her frustrations in conflict. But, instead of taking offence, he chuckled hugely.

'You *have* taken against our traditions, Helena. Why is this? I wonder. Have they affected *you* adversely in some way?' He was too shrewd, or thought he was.

'Not at all,' she said coldly. 'But I've seen what they can do to people I like—Irini and now Chrys.'

'My dear Helena,' he said, at last showing some exasperation, 'do you seriously think that because Chryssanti fancies herself in love with Christos, he should immediately throw aside his plans—plans made many years ago—and marry *her* instead?' He might have been speaking on his own account and Lena bit her lip, which had developed an ominous tendency to tremble.

'No, of course not,' she muttered. 'She's too young to know her own mind. I realise that.'

'Then I fail to see your point.'

'There wasn't one.' Not one that she was prepared to discuss with him anyway. 'Oh, for heaven's sake,' she cried, 'let's drop the subject! We'll never agree.'

'True,' he assented. 'And that is because we come from different cultures. Is that not an argument against mixed marriages, such as Irini's?'

In Irini's case it had proved very successful, Lena thought, but she felt sure Marcos wasn't just thinking of his aunt, and she didn't feel like arguing any more.

'How much longer do we have to stay?' she asked abruptly.

'It would be considered discourteous to leave until the dancing is over. Come,' he smiled and extended his hand to her, 'I believe you do not dislike our dances. That is one tradition you may approve of.'

'I don't feel like dancing. I'll sit and watch.'

'If you do not dance with *me* you will surely be claimed by another partner who will *not* take no for an answer. Many men are watching us with envy.'

Stubbornly, she shook her head.

'I'll take a chance on that.'

'You will not!' The smile had gone and his hand shot out and grasped her arm. 'We Greeks do not like to be refused, and I will not watch you dance with someone else.'

'You've got no right to monopolise me,' she gasped as he pulled her hard into his arms.

'Have I not?' He tilted her chin to look into blue eyes stormy with anger. 'Have I not, Helena?'

'No,' she said more firmly than she felt. 'I don't belong to you.'

'Not yet, perhaps.' His grasp tightened.

What did he mean by 'not yet'? He was betrothed elsewhere. They both knew that. Surely he hadn't got the unmitigated gall to imagine that she would be prepared to have an affair with him? She couldn't very well ask him, and he didn't seem disposed to continue the argument. He seemed content to dance, holding her closely, and with each dance her torment grew. Sexual tension lay between them, sharp as a spur. She could feel his body hardening with desire. The clean, masculine scent of his body assailed her nostrils, and she felt small and helpless in his clasp.

She stumbled slightly and he looked down into her eyes.

'Tired?' he asked, and without waiting for an answer went on, 'Lean on me. I won't let you fall.'

She felt herself getting lost in the dark depths of his eyes and she was achingly aware of his heavy breath as his ribcage rose and fell against her soft breasts. And he knew the effect he was having on her, damn him.

'Please, Marcos,' she pleaded, her voice thick and husky. 'I don't want to dance any more.'

'Very well.' His ready compliance should have made her suspicious. An arm still around her waist, he led her away from the circling couples, away from the lighted square.

'I just meant I wanted to sit down,' she protested as their steps led them up one of the steep, narrow streets, further and further away from the music, the voices and the laughter.

'In a moment,' he soothed.

High above the village, a green olive-clad hill overlooked the flat roofs of the houses, the blue-domed churches and the moonlit harbour. A jagged semicircle of rocks formed a natural shelter. Here, engulfed in the sweet perfume of the herb-covered hillside, Marcos pulled her down beside him on the rustling sun-dried grass. As he gazed into her face, Lena felt her pulses humming in her ears. Slowly, heat suffused her body and she couldn't look away from him. She couldn't seem to think clearly.

'Helena,' he murmured, 'beautiful Helena.' At the sound of his voice, desire flooded her and she began to tremble. She felt her nipples' tingling response as they tightened and thrust against the cotton material of her dress.

'Marcos, I don't think...'

'No,' he agreed, 'don't think, just feel.' His arms circled her then, pulling her into the hard planes of his body, fitting her soft curves to him, to his burgeoning arousal.

With a little defeated moan she closed her eyes and slid her arms around his neck, parting her lips for him. His mouth closed fiercely over hers, claiming it in a hungrily passionate, possessive kiss. His tongue probed, tasting, exciting her, in an erotic simulation of lovemaking.

The kiss went on and on, deepening, growing hotter, more demanding. Marcos's hands found the tiny buttons that fastened her bodice, and his hands slipped inside, cupping her breasts, teasing their budding tips, kneading the soft flesh with his strong fingers. Her body throbbed and burned. Yet some dim instinct prompted her to groan a protest.

'But I *want* to touch you, Helena,' he murmured insistently. 'To touch you, to taste you.' His mouth opened over one swollen nipple, suckling it gently. 'I wanted you from the first moment I saw you,' he muttered against her mouth. 'I tried to hold back until...' He broke off, then, 'But it is no use. I want to make love to you, Helena, now, tonight.'

But, though she ached for him, her head was beginning to clear.

'No, Marcos! No!' She thrust her hands against his shoulders, trying to push him away from her. But he was big and strong.

'You want me too, Helena,' he told her. 'I know you do. Don't insult my intelligence and yours by denying it.'

'All right,' she whispered. 'You can make me want you. I won't deny it. But I'm not going to give in to it. It's not right, Marcos. You're not free and I...'

'If I *were* free,' he probed, 'what then?'

'I don't know. How could I know? You can't theorise about a thing like that.'

'If I were free, you *would* let me make love to you,' he insisted. 'I know it.' His hand brushed along the smooth length of her leg until it reached her thigh. 'Suppose I were to tell you I am not going to marry Marianthe?'

'But you can't tell me that,' she said bitterly, pushing his hand away. 'And if you did I wouldn't believe you. Because you'd only be saying it to get what you want from me.'

CHAPTER SIX

'WELL?' She challenged him as he released her. 'You *can't* tell me that, can you?'

'No.' There was a weary note in the deep voice. 'No, I cannot tell you *that*, Helena. What I *can* tell you is that I will never take from you what you do not give willingly.' He stood up and offered her a helping hand. 'Come, we will return to the dance.'

She ignored the hand, scrambling to her feet unaided.

'I'd rather go back to the villa.' She hadn't far to look for an excuse. 'I'm still anxious about Chrys. I don't think she'll stay in Greece after this. I think she'll want to go home. And *I* shall go with her.' It was said as a kind of test. But Marcos did not react as she'd expected—or hoped?

'Certainly she must not go unaccompanied. But are you sure she cannot be persuaded to stay? My grandfather has accepted her. He will not be pleased if she leaves now.'

'Your grandfather gets too much of his own way,' Lena remarked tartly. 'The way he arranges his family's lives, it's pretty obvious he doesn't know what it's like to be in love.'

'On the contrary.'

'You mean *his* father didn't arrange his marriage for him?'

'It is true his first two marriages were arranged, but...'

'The first *two*! How many times has he been married, for heaven's sake?'

'Three times—first to *my* grandmother—Katarina, then to Tina, Irini's mother. His third wife Rallia was the grandmother of Christos and his brothers. Sadly, Rallia died two years ago.'

'And that marriage was not arranged?'

'No. He was deeply in love with Rallia. For her sake he divorced Tina, antagonising her family, who had once been close friends with the Mavroleons. Now the families are sworn enemies.'

Lena shook her head wonderingly.

'I know he's your grandfather, Marcos, but I must say I think he's an old hypocrite.'

As they returned to the square, the flares had been extinguished and the visitors from the villa had begun to disperse, clattering through the cobbled streets on their donkeys. It was a remarkably attractive sight, the steep setting of narrow alleys on a clear night of moonshine, with dark-shadowed hillside standing over the luminous white of the houses.

Lena and Marcos rode in silence, each immersed in their own thoughts. As they neared the villa, dawn was stealing over the hilltops and vociferous birds greeted the days as the pearly foredawn was rent apart by the streaming rays of the sun.

Chryssanti was asleep when Lena looked in on her. But it was obvious to Lena's keen gaze that the younger girl had cried herself to sleep. Sighing sympathetically over the anguish of love, Lena went to her own room to snatch a few badly needed hours of rest. She woke to find the household in an uproar.

When the Black Lions of Skiapelos lost their tempers, they made it known. As Lena went out on to the patio where the family were assembled for a late breakfast, she found them in a subdued mood, but not because of the previous night's frivolities. From Thalassios's apartments nearby could be heard the sound of raised voices, the words indistinguishable but their mood unmistakable.

'Whatever's going on?' Lena murmured as she slipped into a seat beside Chryssanti.

'Marcos and my grandfather are having a terrible row. It's been going on for ages. But nobody seems to know what it's about.' The girl's mouth trembled and her tawny eyes were anxious. 'Do you think it's about me and…and Christos?' she whispered. 'People seem to tell Grandfather everything. I suppose it was that hateful Dimitri.'

'Not necessarily,' Lena returned, her own voice lowered. 'I told Marcos…I'm sorry, Chrys,' as the girl gave an indignant gasp, 'but I thought he was the best person to ask if Dimitri was telling the truth.'

Chryssanti's whisper became urgent.

'And now Marcos has told my grandfather. Now *everyone* will know. *Christos* will know. I can't stand it. Oh, Lena, how soon can we get away from here?'

But before Lena could confess her ignorance there was a lull in the raging argument. In the sudden silence the family looked at each other with uneasy, speculative eyes.

Then Marcos strode out on to the patio. His rugged features were deeply flushed and drawn into lines of anger. The eloquent black eyes took in the assembled company in one sweeping glance, coming to rest on Lena's face.

'Helena! There you are at last! How long will it take you to pack?'

'Ten minutes. I didn't bring m…'

'Right! Ten minutes, then. We're leaving!'

'But what…?'

'There's no time to discuss it. Not unless you want to be left behind.' He was gone, as rapidly as he'd appeared.

Half-way to her room, Lena found Chryssanti at her heels.

'I'm coming, too. I'm not staying here.'

Lena stopped short. The poor kid. How could she have forgotten Chrys's problems?'

'Oh, Chrys, I ...'

'You heard what Marcos said. There's no time to argue. I'm *coming*!'

Marcos did not seem surprised to find both girls waiting for him.

'What about Stephen?' Lena asked anxiously as Marcos hurried them out to the waiting limousine.

'Stefanos has come home,' Marcos reassured her. 'He is happy and he will be well cared for.'

'But your grandfather doesn't know Chrys is leaving,' Lena worried. 'Will that make any difference to the way he treats Stephen? Won't he be angry?'

Marcos shrugged immaculately tailored shoulders.

'He is already angry. But no, whatever else he is, he is a fair-minded man.' He patted her arm. 'Stop worrying, Helena, the child will be all right.'

'So *you* don't think Chrys ought to stay?'

'I *wouldn't* stay, whatever *he* thought——' Chryssanti began. She still did not like the eldest of her cousins.

'Chryssanti!' Marcos cut sternly across her protest. 'Right or wrong, we seem to be taking you with us. Be satisfied. In any case, in a few weeks you will be of age. In your country that means you may please yourself?'

'Yes.' Despite his tone, Chryssanti was placated. 'My birthday is the same day as Marianthe's. Isn't that a co-incidence, Lena?'

But on *her* birthday Marianthe couldn't do as *she* liked, Lena thought. She had to marry Marcos. But then, perhaps she wanted to.

'You will have Marianthe's company on the voyage,' Marcos said, surprising them both, pleasing Chryssanti and filling Lena with foreboding. 'My great-aunt Arietta,' referring to the nun, 'is also aboard. She wishes to return early to Athens. But we are going to make a detour first, via Marianthe's home. I have to visit her parents.'

Of course. There would be plans to be made for the forthcoming wedding, and the great-aunt would be there to play chaperon. It was just as well—Arietta's presence would also prevent Marcos from paying attention to herself, Lena mused; but it was not a consoling thought. On the contrary.

'I think I'll go straight to my cabin, if you don't mind,' she said tautly. 'I've only had a few hours' sleep every night this week, and the tiredness is catching up with me.' She didn't add, as she might have done, 'with its attendant depression'. And she knew it was not just lack of sleep that was affecting her mood.

There was a very different atmosphere on board from that which had pervaded the outward voyage. Then, everyone had been in high spirits. On the return trip, without exception, the prevailing mood was one of mingled tension and gloom.

Lena knew the reason for her own and Chryssanti's depression. But she could not fathom what lay behind the frame of mind of their three companions. Arietta Mavroleon was aloof and decidedly offhand in her attitude towards everyone. Marianthe's dark, piquant little face was drawn and often her eyes revealed apprehension. As for Marcos... Lena understood him least of all. He too was withdrawn, and there was a brooding impatience about him that would not let him rest, so that he was continuously striding the decks of his yacht.

Since they'd left Skiapelos he had not exchanged more than two words with her, Lena thought miserably. For the sake of her conscience and self-respect she ought to be glad—particularly with his fiancée also on board. But, regardless of these strictures to herself, she missed and ached for his kisses, the caresses that had brought her body to such tingling, vital life.

The day before they reached Mykonos, the *meltemi*, the wild, dry north-east wind, began to blow. At first it only ruffled the hitherto placid water. But at midday the sky paled hotly and the colour of the sea began to darken to an angry blue, whipped into a passion of myriad waves. The *meltemi* blew all day, fretting the sea into more and more ominous behaviour, that made Lena think sympathetically of the perils of the *Odyssey*. The scouring wind kept the *Poseidon*'s passengers below decks.

'It's not a day of *bounatsa*, of goodness,' Marianthe told Lena. 'It's not a day to be on the sea. And now the *meltemi* has come it will blow for days.'

Out of the tearing wind the sun's heat was unabated, and, though at dusk there was a little coolness, it was an illusory refreshment. As the evening wore on, tempers were beginning to fray. Chryssanti was inclined to be tearful, even the gentle-natured Marianthe was heard to snap once or twice. And though her calling demanded patience and resignation Arietta played restlessly with the amber *kombolaki*, or worry beads reminiscent of a rosary, that many Greeks affected.

The warm night bred restlessness in Lena, too, and she began to feel she must escape from the company of

others. With a murmured excuse she stood up and left
the salon and hurried along the carpeted corridors...

'Helena, where are you going?' As she passed the door
to the master-suite, Marcos was just emerging and his
hand on her arm halted her.

'Up on deck.'

'Impossible. It is not safe.'

'I need some air,' she pleaded, 'a change of scenery.
I'm tired of staring at the four walls of that salon, of
the atmosphere in there.'

'We can at least provide the change of scenery.' Before
she'd realised what he was about to do he had drawn
her through the door into the foyer of his suite and thence
into the vast sitting-room. The protest she was about to
make died on her lips as she took in her surroundings.

The yacht was a large one, but even so it had not prepared her for the size or elegance of the owner's accommodation. The sitting-room's vaulted ceiling reached two
decks to a skylight through which the troubled sky could
be seen. The wide expanse of deep carpet led her eye to
an archway which revealed a bedroom beyond, and
before she dragged her unwillingly fascinated eyes away
they had registered the size of the bed and its opulent
coverings.

'Marcos,' she croaked. 'I can't stay. I'll.., I'll go back
to the salon. I...'

'Not yet.' He drew her towards a settee upholstered
in a rich red brocade. 'Sit down!' It was said in a tone
that brooked no denial.

As he sat beside her, she edged away.

'Well, just for a few minutes, then. I really ought...'

'Helena!' He sounded exasperated and his fingers
seized her wrist in an iron grip. 'You have been alone

with me before. Why this sudden nervousness, this un-
willingness for my company?'

Despite his inference Lena was no coward. The time
had come, she felt, for plain speaking.

'Yes, I've been alone with you before. But it shouldn't
have happened, Marcos. It isn't right. I knew it then,
but...'

'But you let me make love to you nevertheless?' His
grasp had gentled and his thumb drew lazy, sensuous
circles on her palm.

'It was wrong of me...wrong of you.' She tried to
pull out of his grasp.

'Then why did you let me kiss you?' he demanded
gently. 'Why did you kiss me in return?' He subjected
her to an eye-contact she could not break.

In desperation, she shook her honey-coloured head
from side to side.

'I don't know. I...'

'Oh, but you do, Helena.' His husky voice held her
in thrall. 'I think we *both* know why. It is because we
recognise something between us that cannot be denied.
A chemistry that, despite all obstacles, draws us into each
other's arms.'

At his words her body tightened and the primal force
within her responded. She felt breathless. Chemistry, yes,
that was all it was to him, while she... It wasn't easy
to think, to be rational, when her every instinct was to
give in to his seduction.

'But that's why we mustn't be alone,' she told him
with a kind of desperation in her voice. 'Don't you see,
if we can't fight it then we must avoid situations where...'
The words trailed off as he moved impatiently towards
her, and her body vibrated its alarm.

'I have no intention of avoiding you, or of avoiding occasions like this,' he said. His gaze swept over her, taking in the simple frock she had worn for dinner, and the firm thrust of her breasts beneath it, and she felt her nipples harden with excitement she could not quell. His sensual inspection moved down over the curves of her waist and hips as intimately as if he were touching her, took in her well-shaped legs, the delicate ankles. As his gaze returned to her face she felt as though she must drown in the liquid allure of his dark eyes. 'I want you, Helena, and you want me,' he said huskily. Moist heat in the most vulnerable part of her body made her shudder, and involuntarily her lips parted. Oh, if only he didn't exude this irresistible sexual magnetism that made nonsense of all her resolutions.

She wondered what it would be like to be beneath him, to have his hands run over her, easing this inner aching, bringing her to the fulfilment she craved. Unaware that she did so, she swayed towards him, and the next moment she was in his arms.

'You see, my Helena, you do not want to resist any more than I do,' he breathed triumphantly before his lips closed over hers. Never had she been so stirred by a man's kiss.

Oh, God! The prayerful thought sped through Lena's bemused brain, but it was ineffective. She had passed beyond redemption. Marcos buried his lips in the hollow of her neck, tasted the sweetness of her skin, and his hands began to move over her body, knowing the flare of her hips, the curved firmness of her buttocks, the straining fullness of her breasts.

She knew how aroused he was when he shuddered violently and pulled her to him almost roughly, adjusting their position so that they lay stretched the full length of the settee. She was aware of every ragged breath he took, aware too of the unashamed, vibrant masculinity that throbbed between them.

'Marcos!' She hardly recognised her own voice. Her utterance of his name was a plea, for him to be strong for both of them. But he misunderstood, taking it for want, for surrender. His kiss, his touch, became more and more erotic, his hands moving lower, seeking greater intimacy.

With a little gasp she gave into her own need to touch him, pressing against him, her hands finding their way beneath his shirt as she knew an aching void that craved to be filled. The skin of his back was warm and damp, and he drew in a long, shuddering breath as her fingers kneaded its muscular breadth.

'Helena!' The urgency of his voice, of his body, told her he'd reached the point where kissing and touching wasn't enough. 'Come into the bedroom,' he urged huskily. 'I want you in my bed—now.'

At his words, a fierce jolt of desire rippled through her. But they brought her also to a realisation of just what she was permitting, of what might happen. They reminded her, too, that *she* had no right in Marcos's bed. That privilege belonged to someone else, to a girl she liked, who didn't deserve to be betrayed this way. She began to struggle.

'No, Marcos!' she panted as he fought her attempts to be free of him. 'For God's sake, think what you're doing.' With the strength of sudden desperation, she wrenched herself out of his arms.

With trembling hands she began to adjust her dress, refastening with difficulty the buttons of which his fingers had made such light work. After one glance she dared not meet his eyes again, but that fleeting glance was enough to show them glazed and clouded with arousal. She was still trembling with reaction. She still wanted him, with as much ferocity as he wanted her, but it was impossible.

Say something, she begged him inwardly, say something to break this awful tension. But he was silent, and it was she who finally spoke again as she moved towards the door.

'I'm sorry, Marcos. I didn't intend... If you remember, I said we shouldn't be alone together. Oh, Marcos!' It was a plea from the heart, and now she did look at him where he lay still half sprawled across the settee. 'Please say you understand, that you agree with me.' He was staring at her with an intensity that unerved her. 'We couldn't... Not when you and Marianthe are...' Her shifting gaze lowered once more, looking anywhere but at his face. Her stomach jolted violently, while a surge of heat suffused her body as her eyes encountered the evidence of his arousal which the taut material of his trousers revealed all too plainly. With a little inarticulate cry, she turned and fled before her resolution could waver.

It would be a relief when this voyage was over. The yacht, which had once seemed so large, was too small to contain both her and Marcos and the strength of the magnetism that sparked between them.

Another white-hot day, and there was Mykonos at last with its guardian windmills that converged on the attractive port. Sundrenched bare hills rose from a deep blue sea, and the air was full of the tingling blend of ozone and pine scent that seemed to typify the Greek seashore.

Marcos planned only a short stay, just long enough to see his future in-laws. But he suggested his passengers came ashore with Marianthe to pay their respects to her parents, and Lena confessed herself curious to see something of the island.

They landed by launch on the crescent of whitewashed shops and cafés. Fishing-boats and small yachts bobbed at anchor or were hauled up on the quay. Here again was the architecture peculiar to the Cyclades: chunky, cubist whitewashed houses with tall, fretted chimneys and pastel-coloured wedding-cake churches dotting the brown landscape. Many of these tiny chapels, Marianthe told Lena, had been built by supplicants who had recovered from a serious illness, or by sailors who had returned home after surviving dangers at sea.

'Thia Arietta,' she said, with a glance at the nun, 'built one of the chapels on Skiapelos in thanksgiving for her vocation.'

They walked up from the quayside, Lena and Marianthe a little ahead of the others. Mykonos was no ethnic Greek community struggling to make a living out of farming and fishing, Lena soon realised. On this island, the tourist trade was *big* business. The crowded, tortuous lanes of the town, as well as the waterfront, were lined with restaurants, bars and boutiques selling various improbable transformations of sponges and seashells.

'It's my home, but,' Marianthe said with a sigh, 'I wish it were not quite so popular with tourists. I'd like it to be more like Skiapelos, quiet and unspoiled.'

'You'll be glad when you go to live there permanently, then,' Lena said. It was an effort to hide her feelings and speak naturally, but she did like this Greek girl, very much, and not for the world would she cause her any pain.

'Oh, no!' Marianthe sounded quite aghast. 'I shan't be living on Skiapelos.'

Of course, silly of her, Lena realised. Marcos's business must keep him in Athens most of the year around. Marianthe would hardly wish to be separated from her husband. Lena knew that, much as *she* had loved his island home, if she were married to Marcos she wouldn't want to spend so much time apart from him. Her insides contracted. She wouldn't want to spend *any* time apart from him.

'But you'll go there quite often to visit, I expect?' she went on doggedly, torturing herself.

'No,' Marianthe said it with quiet regret, 'this was my last visit to the islands.'

'But I don't understand,' Lena puzzled. 'If you're going to marry Marcos...'

'I don't *want* to marry Marcos,' Marianthe muttered fiercely, with an uneasy glance over her shoulder.

Lena stared at her, incredulity mingling with flaring hope.

'But...'

'But I shall have to, unless I can get away.'

'Why don't you just tell him?'

The other girl's olive-skinned face blanched visibly.

'I couldn't do that. I couldn't hurt his feelings. Oh, Lena, will you help me?'

'How can *I* help you?'

'Marcos is going to see my parents today, and the next time he comes here it will be for our wedding. But if I'm not here there won't *be* any wedding. Lena, when the yacht leaves, will you hide me in your cabin? I must get away from my father and get to Athens.'

'Oh, Marianthe, do you think that's wise? Look what happened to Marcos's aunt. Her family disowned her.'

'My mother will be on my side. But even if she wasn't, I wouldn't care. I won't marry someone I don't love. Would *you*?'

'No, but...'

'Then please say you'll help me.'

'Suppose Marcos finds out you're on board?'

'He won't if we're careful.'

'But I share a cabin with Chryssanti.''

'*She* won't give me away. She doesn't like Marcos.'

'Don't *you* like him, Marianthe?'

'Yes,' was the surprising reply. 'I just don't want to marry him. He's too old for me. Besides...' She hesitated, then almost defiantly declared, 'There's someone else.'

Oh, dear, history was repeating itself. Lena looked at the other girl with concern, wondering if Marianthe knew what she was doing. After all, she was only the same age as Chryssanti. She felt she'd like to help the younger girl, but wondered whether she ought to. She couldn't be sure her motive wasn't just one of self-interest.

'Promise me you'll help,' Marianthe interrupted her reflections in an urgent whisper. 'Before the others catch up with us.'

'I'll try,' was as far as Lena would commit herself.

In the event, it was ridiculously easy. As soon as they arrived at the Lychnos's house, Marcos was closeted with his future father-in-law, while Arietta conversed politely with Mrs Lychnos. The three girls were left to their own devices.

'I'm going back on board now,' Marianthe told Lena and Chryssanti. By now Chryssanti had been let into the secret. 'My mother is bound to offer you some refreshments before you leave. If she asks where I am, say you don't know.'

'It was very impolite of Marianthe to disappear without a word of farewell,' Arietta said with displeasure as they made their way back to the yacht.

Lena pretended not to see Chryssanti's knowing look. Besides, she was more interested in Marcos's reaction than in that of his aunt. It was as well Marianthe had made herself scarce almost immediately, because Marcos had not remained long with her father. He had emerged grim-faced and had declined Mrs Lychnos's offer of refreshment.

As they walked back down the hill to the quayside, Lena stole furtive glances at Marcos's profile. He looked almost as angry as he had done after the quarrel with his grandfather. She was consumed by curiosity, and grateful when Arietta asked, 'Are all the arrangements in hand for the wedding?'

But she was not as gratified by Marcos's curt affirmative. But then, he did not know of Marianthe's plans. So why the anger, then?

On board, Lena made an excuse to go straight to her cabin, where a nervous Marianthe awaited her.

'I'll have to hide in the bathroom,' she told Lena.

'But suppose one of the stewards comes to clean up?'

In the end it was decided that Lena should feign an indisposition and keep to her cabin for the short time it would take them to sail back to Piraeus. Once back in the home port, Marianthe would stay in hiding until Marcos and his party were safely departed.

'What will you do then?' Lena asked.

'It's better you don't know too much. But don't worry. I have a friend in Athens. We were at school together in Paris. She'll help me.'

'Are you quite recovered?' Marcos asked Lena as the limousine bore them swiftly back towards Athens, and guiltily she nodded her thanks. 'If you come and see me at the office tomorrow, we will talk about a job for you.'

'Oh, no!' Lena exclaimed. 'I mean, it's very good of you, but you've obviously forgotten I have to go back to England with Chrys.'

'I forget nothing. Thia Arietta will accompany Chryssanti. She wishes to see Irini and perhaps bring her some religious comfort in her illness.'

'Oh, good!' Lena said impulsively. She turned to the nun. 'Do you have any messages for Irini from her father?'

Arietta shook her head.

'My brother was in no mood to send messages when we left Skiapelos. In any case, he does not forgive easily.'

'You won't tell Irini that?' Lena pleaded, and for a moment the nun's stern face softened.

'I believe you are a good-hearted girl, *thespinis*. No, you have my promise that I will be tactful.'

'So you see, Lena,' Marcos put in, 'there is no reason why you should not remain in Athens.'

Only one, perhaps—that to stay might mean getting hurt. But, even so, she could not bring herself to pass up this opportunity of seeing Marcos for a little longer.

'So I'm going to accept the job whatever it is,' she wrote to Sally in a long delayed letter that evening. 'I may be a fool, but I know he's sexually attracted to me, and with Marianthe determined not to marry him, perhaps there's a chance for me, after all.' Biting her pen in thought, she looked out across the roof garden towards the floodlit Acropolis, and wondered fancifully if the old gods and goddesses were on her side. A thought occurred to her, and she bent to her task once more. 'At least one good thing has come out of this. I'm totally over Petros. In fact, I can't think what I ever saw in him.' She ended with her best wishes to Domenicos Theodopoulos and the message that she would be writing him a separate letter concerning her errand to Thalassios Mavroleon.

'As you have had office experience, I am putting you to work with my secretary,' Marcos told Lena next day. She had only volunteered the information that she could do shorthand and typing. 'We are in the middle of some very important negotiations at present, and Lydia is extremely busy. Though you know nothing about oil or shipping contracts, it is merely a matter of copy-typing and perhaps taking a few letters at my dictation.'

Lena hid a smile as she confirmed that she would be equal to such a task.

'The work need only be part-time, if you wish,' Marcos went on, 'so that you can continue with your sightseeing.'

But over the next few days she was kept too fully occupied. And she didn't really mind. Somehow the idea of sightseeing had palled. And there was a satisfaction, too, in being back in a world she knew so well, even though she was careful not to reveal the fact.

Chryssanti was tearful when Lena saw her and Arietta Mavroleon off at the airport. For a moment or two she clung to Lena.

'Write to me, won't you?' Then, 'I'm scared, Lena. Scared how I'll find Mum. And it's terrible to think I'll never see Christos again.'

'Chrys...' Lena hesitated. She didn't want to appear to preach, and Chryssanti would probably resent it. But perhaps, later on, when time had faded the hurt a little, the younger girl would remember Lena's advice and be glad of it. 'Chrys, you're still very young. You'll fall in love again some day. Meanwhile, why not carry on with your studies and think about a career? Try and forget about Christos,' she urged.

'It's all right for *you*,' Chryssanti retorted. 'Marianthe doesn't want to marry Marcos. *You* stand a chance, especially working with him.'

Lena hadn't realised her feelings were so transparently obvious, and if they were obvious to Chryssanti, what about Marcos himself?

But working for Marcos was not bringing Lena any closer to him. Since they had been back in Athens he had withdrawn into a reserve which both puzzled and piqued her. Any conversation between them was concerned purely with office routine.

'I'm beginning to think I know more about the Mavroleon Shipping Company than I do about Marcos,' she wrote in another bulletin to Sally. 'It's certainly run on a much larger scale than Theodopoulos's. The funny thing is, they seem to do business with every Greek company based in London *except* Theodopoulos's. I suppose it has something to do with the feud Domenicos mentioned between him and old Thalassios. I wonder what it was about?'

She had been working for Marcos just over a week when he called her into his office. Thinking he wanted to dictate some letters, she carried a notebook and pen and sat in the chair facing him, waiting expectantly.

He was frowning over a letter on his desk and he did not look up for a long time, giving her an opportunity, lacking of late, to study him. He looked tired, she thought. His rugged face seemed more lined than usual about the brow and eyes, and she was certain there were new signs of grey at his hairline. The normally sensual curves of his mouth were drawn into a grim line. As she studied him, she knew he had lost none of his attraction for her, and her insides twisted painfully as she recalled the times he had kissed and caressed her. But his wedding day was less than two weeks away, and obviously that accounted for his recent restraint. She wondered what would happen when he found out his promised bride had vanished. Would he be hurt? Her heart yearned over him in a longing to show him he did not need Marianthe.

Unknowingly, her eyes were still filled with liquid feeling when he looked up and caught her gaze on him. She heard him draw in a sharp breath and his lips tightened still more. Abruptly he stood up and came round the desk towards her. A profound elemental need stirred within her, and, as her body throbbed, she swallowed and passed her tongue surreptitiously over her lips.

She couldn't have moved if she'd wanted to—and she didn't want to. She hadn't been this close to him in days. He was so close, she could see every one of the individual hairs on the back of his hand as it grasped the letter, and she had to restrain her own fingers from reaching out to touch him.

'Helena!'

She looked up into his face and felt her heart accelerate.

'Marcos?' she croaked.

His hand moved towards her and her heart thudded painfully in her ears, making her feel giddy. But he did not touch her. Instead he threw the letter into her lap.

'What do you know about this?'

CHAPTER SEVEN

'WHAT is it?' Her eyes were still locked with his.

'Read it!'

Reluctantly she looked down at the letter and scanned its contents. It was from Marianthe's father, reporting that his daughter had mysteriously vanished. The letter was angry rather than distraught. It seemed to be blaming Marcos for the disappearance.

'But *we* know this is not true,' Marcos said when Lena tentatively mentioned it. 'What we do know is that she disappeared the very day we returned her to Mykonos. Too much of a coincidence to be ignored, I think?' He paused, then, tautly, 'What have you said to her, Helena?'

'Me? Said to her? I don't know what you mean.' But she did know that her cheeks were flushed with a guilty stain.

'This is too important for lies, Helena.' His rugged face was stern. 'Marianthe is a young and vulnerable child. I will not have her hurt. What have you told her about us?'

'Nothing!' Lena retorted indignantly. She stood up. 'There was nothing to tell.'

He gave a grunt of incredulity. 'Nothing! You call it nothing what there is between us?'

'Yes,' she said defiantly, though the denial made her heart ache. 'Because there *is* nothing. We both know you're betrothed to Marianthe. All right, once or twice in the heat of the moment we've both behaved very badly.

I'm not excusing myself either. And I certainly wouldn't have told Marianthe about it. It's not something I'm exactly proud of.'

'You wouldn't have told her even in the hope that our engagement might be broken off?' He sounded more curious than condemnatory, but Lena was incensed.

'Certainly not! How can you think I'd be so despicable? And what good would that do *me*?'

'You do not *care* that I am not free to marry you?' It was difficult to gauge his expression. And of course she cared, but it behoved her not to let him know it.

'I only care because it makes *my* behaviour even more despicable,' she told him. 'But I've sworn it won't ever happen again.'

He made an incomprehensible sound in his throat. Then, 'I have your word of honour that you have not revealed any of this to my fiancée?'

'Yes.'

'And you have no idea where she may be?'

'I . . .' Lena was not a good liar and, despite her efforts to sustain it, her gaze fell before his, a pink flush once more staining her cheeks. He pounced in triumph, his hands grasping her shoulders.

'So you have been indulging in sophistry.' Angry now, he gave her a little shake. 'You have told the truth only as far as it suits you. You *do* know something.' He repeated the shake. 'I insist that you tell me.'

It wasn't fear of his anger that was making her legs sag, that made it difficult to swallow.

'I . . . I gave my word, Marcos. I promised,' she managed to say. 'Don't make me break that promise,' she pleaded with him.

'Helena!' He gave her another shake, but it was not as violent and it seemed to bring her closer to him. 'I do not think you realise the seriousness of this. You are not in England now. In Greece, the disappearance of a young unmarried girl is a cause of great concern to her family.'

'And to her fiancé, obviously,' she reminded him tautly.

'As you say.' His own tone was crisp. 'Naturally I am concerned. Now, let us have no more of this nonsense about keeping promises. Where is she?'

'I . . . I don't know exactly,' Lena confessed. 'She hid on board the *Poseidon* until we got back to Piraeus. She said she had a girlfriend here in Athens. She was going to stay with her.'

'Thank God for that!' Marcos exclaimed with a relief that was obviously heartfelt. He *cared* about Marianthe, Lena thought miserably, and that made his behaviour over the past weeks a cynical betrayal, not only of his fiancée, but of *her* too. She stifled a threatening sob.

'Oh, and she said this friend had been at school with her in Paris.' There was no point now in holding back any details.

'Presumably she also told you why she was leaving home without her parents' permission?'

Lena firmed her lips, but not just to still their tendency to tremble. Wild horses wouldn't drag that piece of information from her. That was for Marcos to find out for himself—if Marianthe had the courage to tell him.

'I can't tell you any more.'

'But you *know*.' His dark liquid gaze held hers, daring her to deny it. His hands were still gripping her shoulders, and they stared at each other for an interminable moment. Then something in the quality of the silence changed. She heard and saw Marcos draw in a long, deep breath as his gaze travelled over her. All at once the neat blue summer dress she had worn to work seemed inadequate protection. Her eyes widened and sharp little needles of longing darted through her.

She breathed in the warm masculine scent of him and swallowed hard. She wanted him to pull her closer and bend his head to hers. She wanted him to kiss her and press her soft body against his. She imagined him cupping her breasts, then slipping his fingers beneath the material to tease her nipples. Then he would pick her up and carry her... Carry her where? They were in his office and—besotted fool that she was—that mesmeric quality of his had blinded and deafened her once more to their surroundings and to the impossibility of any relationship between them.

With a little choking sound of protest, she pulled free of him. She took a deep, steadying breath.

'Well,' she challenged him, 'I've told you what you want to know. Hadn't you better start looking for your fiancée?'

There was another of those long silences, then, 'Yes,' Marcos said with heavy finality. 'Yes, I have to find her.'

'I'll get back to work, then.' She turned away, trying to sound bright and matter-of-fact.

'No.' The harsh monosyllable halted her. 'You are coming with me.'

'*Me?*' she squeaked in dismay. 'Why do you want *me*?'

For an instant the corner of his mouth flexed, but he made no direct answer. He picked up the telephone.

'I am going to call Kyrios Lychnos and find out the names and addresses of Marianthe's schoolfriends.'

'And when you find her—if you find her—what then?'

'Naturally I shall take her back to her parents.'

And then no doubt the truth would come out and the marriage date would be brought forward. Lena hadn't been too keen on what she'd seen of Mr Lychnos. He struck her as being a typical domestic tyrant.

'What will they do to her?'

Marcos's gaze softened as it rested on Lena's anxious face.

'Don't worry.' His craggy features actually broke into a smile. 'We Greeks do not beat our women. We have too much respect for them. We protect them.' His voice deepened and his eyes became smoky as he met Lena's own blue gaze. 'We *cherish* them.' He fell into a long, contemplative silence in which his eyes never left hers. Then he seemed to recall himself. 'But she will be severely reprimanded,' he went on briskly, 'and a closer watch will be kept on her for the future.'

'Until she's married and her husband can keep an eye on her?'

'Exactly.'

An hour later, Lena and Marcos stood on the steps of a palatial villa on the outskirts of Athens.

'I feel awful about this,' Lena muttered as a servant unquestioningly ushered them into a large salon where the family and their guest were seated. Apparently, the name Mavroleon was a sure passport to any Greek establishment.

'Lena?' A startled Marianthe came to her feet, then, belatedly, saw Marcos two paces behind. 'Oh, Lena!' Surprise turned to reproach, and the hand she had extended fell to her side. 'How could you?'

'I'm sorry,' Lena began, but the younger girl's face was closed and hostile.

'I thought you were my friend. I'll never forgive you for this.'

Marcos, meanwhile, was in earnest conversation with Marianthe's host and hostess, who, it transpired, had no idea Marianthe was visiting their daughter without her parents' knowledge and consent. Nor did Lena's part in her escapade pass without censure, even though Marcos spoke in mitigation of her offence.

'Helena is not yet accustomed to our ways.' He obviously believed what he said, and his rider made Lena feel even more guilty. 'She did not realise what she was doing.'

From the outset it was obvious Marianthe's cause was lost, as her friend's parents expressed their shock and concurred with Marcos that she must return home at once. And who better to take charge of her than her fiancé?

There was an uncomfortable silence as the limousine bore Marianthe, a silent, unhappy prisoner, back to the Mavroleon offices. Several times Lena looked at her pleadingly, wanting the other girl to understand she'd had no choice but to reveal her whereabouts. But Marianthe stolidly avoided her gaze.

Back in his office, Marcos telephoned the Lychnos family, then gave instructions for his private helicopter to be on stand-by.

'I may be away for several days,' he told his secretary. 'Helena...' He paused by her desk. And for a moment she thought he was going to say something important. Then, with a little shrug, 'I will speak to you when I get back.' With a curt nod he was gone, his hand on Marianthe's elbow, propelling her before him as if he were afraid that even now she would somehow escape him.

When he got back he would probably be a married man, Lena thought dully, and resolved she would not be in Athens to see it.

Lydia, Marcos's secretary, was startled when Lena hinted that she might be leaving Athens shortly.

'Oh, dear, I was hoping that you would be with us for at least another month. You've picked up the work remarkably quickly. One might almost think you've done something similar before. I've found your help invaluable. Especially since this new deal with America is involving us in so much more paperwork than usual. Couldn't you see your way to staying on a little longer?' she pleaded, and Lena felt it would be churlish and ungrateful to refuse.

Lena had expected the days of Marcos's absence to be long and tedious, but she and Lydia were so busy that the moments fairly flew. They worked long hours, often well past their normal time, as did Marcos's three cousins, Christos, Manoli and Dimitri. And often when Lena returned to her apartment she took work home with her.

It was obvious to Lena, when Christos asked cheerfully but casually after Chryssanti, that he had not guessed at the younger girl's feelings for him. Dimitri, his elder brother, showed more concern, gravely assuring Lena that he had only spoken to Chryssanti with her own welfare in mind.

'Christos has a friendly way with him that might be misconstrued. I felt bound to warn her of his impending marriage. But,' he sighed, 'she resents me now, of course?'

'I'm afraid so,' Lena told him.

The ramifications of the American deal were vast and extremely confidential. It would be a disaster if the

Mavroleons' competitors got to hear of it, Lydia told Lena.

'A great amount of money is at stake.'

'You wouldn't think the Mavroleons would *need* any more money,' Lena said. 'They live like princes now.'

'They live well,' Lydia agreed, 'but it is not just the money. To a Greek businessman it is a matter of prestige. Also they are heavily involved in charitable work. If this deal goes through they will be able to do so much more for their less fortunate countrymen.'

Marcos had been away just over a week when Lena, returning home even later than usual, found lights on all over the penthouse suite. Fearing an intruder, she was just about to re-enter the lift and summon the security guard from his post downstairs when she heard a familiar voice.

'Is that you, Lena?'

Incredulously, she walked back into the apartment, put down her heavy briefcase and stared at the towel-clad figure obviously just emerged from the shower.

'Petros! What on earth are *you* doing here?'

'This *is* my uncle's apartment,' he reminded her. Then, 'How are you, Lena?' He came towards her, and before she could prevent him he pulled her into his arms and kissed her. Automatically her brain registered the fact that his kiss left her quite unmoved, and she thrust him away from her.

'Don't, Petros! And you still haven't explained why you're here.'

'Oh, this and that.' Petros's education and many years in England meant that he spoke excellent colloquial English. He shrugged. 'Some business, but mainly to see you.'

'To see me? What on earth for?'

'Sit down, relax, and I'll explain.'

'When you've dressed,' she suggested pointedly.

'What?' He looked down at himself. 'Oh. Heavens, Lena, I'm decent. And we *were* engaged once.' Even so, she'd never seen him wearing so little.

'I'd still rather you got dressed,' she insisted. 'You never know, I might have a visitor, and I wouldn't want anyone to find you here like this. They might misunderstand.'

'Boyfriend?' he queried, and, at her mute silence and expressive look, 'Oh, all right, I'll throw some clothes on. Quite honestly,' he grumbled, as he retired into one of the spare bedrooms, 'I thought you'd be more pleased to see me than this.'

'I can't think why.' She tossed the words over her shoulder as she went into the kitchen to plug in the coffee percolator.

He followed her a moment later, still barefoot and clad only in his trousers.

'You were in love with me, weren't you? Surely...'

'That seems a very long time ago.'

'Six weeks? A long time?' Then his outraged expression turned to one of smug conceit. 'Of course, it *would* seem a long time, if you were missing me.'

'I haven't missed you a bit,' Lena retorted with more truth than tact as she banged two mugs down on to the worktop. 'I suppose you'd like a coffee?'

'Well, *I've* missed *you*, I can tell you.' At her look of disbelief, he went on, 'Look, Lena, I'm here to apologise. You might make it a bit easier for me.'

'Petros,' she told him, 'I don't care whether you apologise or not.'

'Then you *have* forgiven me?' he said eagerly, moving closer as he spoke. 'You see, I thought I was in love with Eva. But almost as soon as you'd gone I realised...'

'Hold on,' Lena interrupted. 'If you're about to tell me you want me back, you may as well save your breath.'

'But I *do* want you back. I can't believe you've forgotten two years in just a few weeks.'

'I haven't forgotten, Petros. But I've realised I was mistaken in thinking what I felt for you was love—at least, not the love that lasts a lifetime.' She drained the contents of her cup. 'And now, if you'll excuse me, I'm very tired. I've been working very long hours lately.' She moved towards the kitchen door, but Petros made no attempt to move.

'Yes, I heard you were working for the Mavroleons.'

'How...? Oh, Sally, I suppose.' The two girls were still exchanging letters at regular intervals.

'How does it compare with working for my uncle?'

'It's a much larger firm, of course.' Again she made an unsuccessful attempt to bypass him.

'And how do you like the Mavroleons themselves?'

'Very much. Look, Petros, I've got to get up early in the morning. I really must ask you to leave.'

'Leave?' He sounded astonished. 'Why should I leave? I always use Domenicos's apartment when I come to Athens.'

'I don't remember you ever coming here,' Lena retorted. 'Not since *I've* known you, anyway. Domenicos always handled the Athens end himself.'

'Well, this time he's sent me.'

'But I'm here alone. You *can't* stay. It isn't...'

'Oh, for heaven's sake, Lena, you're surely not trying to preach propriety? We *were* going to be married.'

'You can hardly expect that to be a recommendation,' she commented tartly.

'Oh, look!' He put his hands on her shoulders and adopted his winning little-boy smile that once she'd found so appealing. 'I *knew* that must still be rankling with you. But I've said I'm sorry. Can't we kiss and make up?'

'No.' The touch of his hands meant nothing to her. All she could think of was how she felt when Marcos held her this way. Petros, with his blue eyes and blond good looks—rare in a Greek—seemed vapid and colourless when she contrasted him with Marcos.

Petros's hands dropped to his sides. But, 'You'll change your mind in a day or two,' he said confidently, 'when we've seen a bit more of each other. It will be just how it used to be.'

'I don't intend to see any more of you. And if you're not leaving, then *I* must. It's too late now, but tomorrow I'll find somewhere else.' She would ask Lydia's help. The other girl had a large apartment. Surely she wouldn't mind putting Lena up for the remainder of her time in Athens?

Lena slept badly that night. She locked her bedroom door, something she'd never bothered to do when she'd had the apartment to herself. But as far as she knew Petros made no attempt to disturb her.

She rose early. She'd meant to look through some important papers before she went to bed, but instead she had done her packing and written a letter to Sally, telling her to address all future correspondence to her at the Mavroleon office. Now she'd have to read the papers over breakfast. But her plans were frustrated again. Petros was already up and in a determinedly talkative mood which lasted throughout her hasty meal.

'What sort of work are you doing for the Mavroleons?' he asked as he lounged indolently in an armchair. 'The same as you did for us?'

'No. I'm just assisting the managing director's PA.'

'Which one of them *is* managing director these days, now the old man's retired?'

'Marcos Mavroleon.' Just to say his name was exquisite pain.

'Anything interesting going on?'

'Petros, you know better than that. My work is strictly confidential—as it was when I worked for your uncle.' She pushed back her chair. 'I'll find somewhere else to stay and come back for my luggage.'

'There's no need for you to move out,' he grumbled.

'There's every need,' she contradicted him. She picked up her handbag, then looked around her. 'Have you seen my briefcase? Oh, there it is.' She retrieved it from where it lay almost concealed under Petros's armchair. 'I'm off now, and please—once I've moved out, don't try to see me again.'

She didn't wait for his answer, but hurriedly left the apartment, already ten minutes later than she'd intended.

Lydia was most sympathetic when Lena explained that it was no longer convenient for her to use her friend's apartment.

'Of course you must move in with me. To save time, since we're so busy, why don't I send a man to collect your luggage and take it to my place?'

That would avoid another awkward encounter with Petros. Lena agreed, wrote the address on a scrap of paper and handed over her key.

Of necessity, Lydia dealt with all telephone calls, and Lena had given up trying to understand the rapid interchange. After one particularly lengthy call, Lydia reported, 'That was Kyrios Marcos. He returns to Athens tomorrow.'

'Oh?' Lena tried to sound only casually interested. 'Did . . . did he mention Marianthe Lychnos?'

'No. Our conversation was all of business,' Lydia said apologetically. 'Kyrios Marcos will be in the office for a few hours only. Then he flies to America for the final negotiations of the contract. So all these papers must be completed before we leave here tonight.'

Lena had little time that evening to appreciate the comfort of Lydia's apartment. Both girls were so tired, they went straight to bed. Apart from a few necessities, Lena did not even unpack the suitcases brought over from the Theodopoulos apartment.

When Marcos arrived at the Mavroleon corporation next morning, he called Lydia into his office for a consultation, sparing only an abstracted smile and a word of greeting for Lena before he left as hurriedly as he'd arrived.

'Before leaving for America I have to go to Skiapelos—an urgent summons from my grandfather,' he told them.

'Now the contract typing is finished, I suppose I might as well leave,' Lena said to Lydia during the most relaxed lunch hour they'd had for days.

'Finished?' Lydia laughed. 'That was just the preliminary work. Once the Americans have agreed our terms— and that is not certain yet—there will be vast amounts of correspondence.'

'I guessed that, of course.' Lena was still careful not to reveal her familiarity with the shipping firm's procedures. 'But you'll be able to cope now, won't you?'

'I suppose you want to go on with your sightseeing?'

'No,' Lena said slowly, 'I think I might go back to England.' At least there would no longer be any embarrassment in encountering Petros.

'I was hoping,' Lydia said, 'and I think Kyrios Marcos was hoping, too—that you would stay on and let me train you to take my place. You see,' as Lena looked at her enquiringly, 'I hope to be married at the beginning of next year, but I promised not to leave until a replacement was found.'

It was impossible, of course—though for a moment or two Lena let herself be tempted by the idea. To be Marcos's personal assistant. To work closely with him all day, every day. But no, she shook her head; it would be too sweet a torture.

'Don't make up your mind yet,' Lydia begged. 'At least wait until Kyrios Marcos can talk to you about it first. I'm sure he'll make it worth your while to stay.'

Except that there was only one incentive he could offer, and he wasn't free to do so. Even so, she decided weakly, she would stay just a little longer, see him just once more—one more memory to carry home with her.

A day or two later, Lena was taking advantage of the slack period at the office to catch up on some personal shopping. The slender wardrobe she had brought with her from England badly needed replenishing, and she was also beginning to think in terms of souvenirs to take home.

The boutiques were wickedly expensive, but Lena had saved most of her wages and she was in a mood to treat herself. She was trying on several dresses in one of the more exclusive shops when she heard a familiar voice coming from the adjoining cubicle.

'I'll take all of them. I didn't have time to get a proper trousseau, so my husband told me to get anything I wanted.'

Peeping furtively around the curtain of her cubicle, Lena saw Marianthe emerge in the wake of a beaming assistant whose arms were laden with garments. And, as the younger girl wrote a cheque with an air of pretty insouciance, Lena saw the flash of a wedding ring.

She went hot and cold. Nausea rose in her throat. She swayed and clutched at the corner of the booth for support. It was as she'd feared. Marianthe's escapade had resulted in the ceremony being brought forward. Marcos and Marianthe were married, and from the way Marianthe had spoken, the proud lilt in her voice when she mentioned her 'husband', it sounded as if her objections had been easily overcome.

Greek girls, of course, were very carefully protected. It was unlikely that Marcos had ever attempted to make love to his fiancée in the way he had tried to make love to Lena. Marianthe's reluctance might have stemmed from ignorance. Once married to Marcos and subjected to his compelling masculinity, how could she fail to be won over?

You fool, she told herself. So what's different? You *knew* it was going to happen. But the sick feeling would not go away.

The dresses Lena was trying on had lost all their appeal, but she remained where she was, waiting until Marianthe had departed. Just at that moment it would have taken more courage than Lena felt she possessed to face the other girl.

'You have decided, *thespinis*?' The voice of the salesgirl made Lena start.

'Oh...no...yes. That is...I'll take this one.' 'This one' happened to be the one she was wearing at the moment. Without another glance at it, Lena slipped it over her head and handed it to the assistant. Having paid for her purchase, she left the shop and went straight back to Lydia's flat. From there, she telephoned the office and pleaded an indisposition. By this time it was perfectly true. She had a raging headache.

Lydia was concerned.

'And I will not be home until late this evening. I am dining with my fiancé. I could cancel...'

'No!' Lena said hurriedly. The thought of having the apartment to herself was an appealing one. It meant she wouldn't have to put on a cheerful expression for the other girl's benefit, and by the time Lydia returned she would be in bed. 'You've been so busy, you haven't seen your fiancé for ages. I'll be perfectly all right by myself.'

'You *will* be in the office tomorrow?' Lydia asked. 'Kyrios Marcos is returned from Skiapelos. There is much work to be done while he is away in America.'

Lena was relieved she had decided to go straight to the apartment. But tomorrow she would have to face him, and without betraying her mood.

'Yes, I'll be in.'

'I told him I had spoken to you about taking my job here. He seemed very...'

'I can't, Lydia!' Lena interrupted. 'Please, you must tell him I can't possibly stay. I've decided to go back to England.' To the sound of Lydia's dismay, she put the telephone down.

CHAPTER EIGHT

To PASS the dreary evening that followed her discovery, Lena decided to catch up on some personal correspondence. She'd been so busy, she hadn't written to her parents lately. They would be glad to know she was coming home, and so would Sally. She would write to Chryssanti as well and bring her up to date with Marianthe's affairs. Perhaps it would help Lena herself to come to terms with Marcos's marriage to have to put it down in black and white.

She passed a sleepless night, and it was a wan-faced, hollow-eyed Lena who went into work next day, intending only to collect her personal belongings and hand in her notice. But she arrived to find the normally well-ordered office in confusion.

There was no sign of Lydia who, to Lena's surprise, had not returned to the apartment last night. Greek girls, even those who were engaged, did not stay out all night with their fiancés. Through the open door into the adjoining office she saw, not Marcos, but Dimitri Mavroleon.

'Lena, thank goodness! We were not sure if you would be in. Are you recovered?' He looked doubtfully at her drawn features. 'Lydia and her fiancé were involved in an accident last night, and so...'

'Are they all right? They're not...?'

'No, no. Both are fine. Just suffering from bruises and shock. They are staying at her fiancé's home for a day or two. But listen, Marcos has been called away again—back to Skiapelos. Our grandfather is not well.'

'I'm so sorry.'

Dimitri nodded a grave acceptance.

'Before Marcos went, he left instructions that only you were to handle some confidential typing. I will be keeping his appointments for the next few days, which means I am off to America in two hours' time.'

Also in Marcos's drawer, Lena discovered, was a square white envelope addressed to her. At first she thought it might be further instructions, but then she realised the handwriting was unfamiliar. By now she was well acquainted with Marcos's firm, upright script. She studied the envelope, aware of an unreasonable feeling of unease that made her reluctant to open it.

But this was ridiculous. What possible harm could it contain? She slit it open and drew out the single sheet of white cardboard, then drew in her breath in an anguished hiss. It was coincidence, of course. She couldn't really have had a premonition of the pain it would cause her. The card read:

'Mr and Mrs M Mavroleon invite Miss Lena Thomas to a dinner party to celebrate their recent marriage.' There followed the venue, date and time. There was a personal note inscribed on the back. 'Do come. I want to apologise. Marcos has explained everything. Marianthe.'

She couldn't go, of course. Lena sat down in Marcos's chair and leaned on his desk, head in hands, fighting back tears. She couldn't go.

But, after the first blow, a few moments' reasoned thought told her she *must* go and be seen to be unaffected by Marcos's marriage—seen particularly by Marcos himself.

Lydia telephoned next day, sounding none the worse for her experience, but confirmed that she would not return to work until the following week.

'There are some things I haven't been able to deal with,' Lena told her worriedly. 'Things I can't make a decision about. Dimitri's keeping all Marcos's appointments, Christos is always in meetings, and heaven knows where Manoli's been all week. And I didn't like to ask any of the other secretaries. I think they all resent me working for Marcos.'

'You must forgive them,' Lydia laughed. 'They are all a little in love with him.'

'That won't do them much good,' Lena said with caustic fellow-feeling.

'No,' Lydia chuckled again. 'Not now. But leave everything until after the weekend. I will be back then.'

The dinner party was being held at Anastasia's villa that weekend. Lena supposed that a family party as sizeable as the Mavroleons would scarcely fit into Marcos's town house.

At least she had a new dress for the occasion, Lena thought wryly as she dressed that Saturday evening. Despite her hurried, uncaring decision in the boutique, she had chosen well. The soft, midnight-blue cotton with its deep neckline clung alluringly to her slender figure, outlining breast and hip and swirling softly at knee-length to reveal and set off slender, shapely legs. With the golden tan she had acquired she needed no make-up other than a moisturiser, a hint of blue eyeshadow and a soft pink lipstick that enhanced the full, soft lines of her mouth.

She had ordered a taxi to take her out to the villa, and she was just applying a mist of soft, subtle perfume when the doorbell rang. She snatched up her handbag and a light wrap. The evenings were growing cooler now that the end of summer was approaching. As the bell repeated its summons, she hurried to the door.

But it was no taxi driver who confronted her.

'Marcos!' His name was a startled gasp on her lips, and instinctively she drew back, not wanting him near her with the disastrous effect his proximity would have. But he was so handsome in his evening clothes, he took her breath away.

'Who were you expecting?' he demanded, a suspicious note in his voice.

'No one... At least... that is... I ordered a taxi.'

'I sent a message that I would pick you up.'

'I didn't get it. But Marcos, there was no need for you... Surely you should be at...'

'Of course there is a need. You are *my* guest. Come!' He stretched out a peremptory hand, but deftly she avoided his touch and preceded him out of the apartment and into the lift.

'Surely Marianthe will think it very strange that you...'

'Why should she?' He sounded genuinely puzzled. 'And what does it matter? She has other things to occupy her than wondering how I spend *my* time.'

Lena was speechless. How could a newly married man speak so casually of his wife? Couldn't he see how odd it looked that he should be fetching another woman to his dinner party? Especially a woman to whom, it had been proved, he was not sexually indifferent.

'You look very lovely, Helena,' he commented as he ushered her into the lift. 'But then, you always do.' His gaze swept over her, taking in the exquisite blue dress, the firm thrust of her breasts beneath it. The clinging skirt enhanced the curves of her waist and hips. It was as if mentally he was undressing her, and she was aware that the exercise was disturbing him. Finally, his eyes connected with hers and held. As always, she reacted to his hypnotic stare. She couldn't seem to look away from him. His gaze had moved to her mouth now. The result was like a physical caress. Her lips parted and she drew in her breath sharply, knowing that she must dispel the sensual tension that had sprung between them.

It was difficult in the small service lift to distance herself from him. Tall, long-legged, broad of shoulder, he seemed to fill the enclosed space, the warmth, the scent, the male aura of him. Lena felt heat spread through her abdomen and wondered if her face was flushed.

'H—how is your grandfather?' she asked. She genuinely wanted to know, but the question broke the sensual spell he had cast upon her.

'Much recovered thank you. Fortunately it was only a slight heart attack, brought on by a fit of anger.' He added grimly, 'I am afraid it was my fault. We quarrelled again. The doctor says that in future he must not be worried with business or family affairs, or he cannot answer for the consequences.' Marcos sounded suddenly weary, and Lena guessed such cares would now fall to *his* responsibility.

'Here we are.' His hand at her waist, he ushered her into the back of his limousine, following her far too closely for comfort. 'Kyria Tassia's house, Spyros, *parakalo*,' he told the chauffeur.

'You are quite recovered from the other day?' Marcos asked as the limousine drew away. His voice was full of deep concern. 'I was sorry not to see you before I left.

Lydia felt guilty. She said maybe she had let you overdo things. You are not used to working in our climate.'

Lena seized on the excuse.

'That's one of the reasons I'm thinking of going home.' But as she said it depression gripped her.

'Yes, Lydia said you had turned down the chance of taking her job. She said you sounded almost frightened on the telephone, that you spoke of returning to England. I had hoped you would change your mind about that.'

Lena shook her head, not trusting herself to look at him. She was aware of a very strong desire to burst into tears.

'Do not worry, Helena!' There was amusement in his voice, and he leaned towards her, placing a hand on her knee. 'I do not want you to take the job.'

'You . . . you don't?' For a moment, surprise mingled with a sense of chagrin banished all other emotions and she was able to look at him.

'No. I have already found a suitable replacement for Lydia.' As his gaze met hers, his dark eyes kindled into liquid fire. 'No,' he repeated, 'I have something quite different in mind for you, *mikros ena mou*.'

At his words, at the endearment, violent tremors shuddered through Lena's body. She wanted to look away, but his expression compelled her, held her mesmerised. She shouldn't be alone with him like this. It was too dangerous. The chauffeur behind his smoked-glass screen didn't count. Marcos shouldn't be looking at her like this. He shouldn't be about to kiss her. As his head came nearer, the limousine's telephone rang. The spell broken, she jerked away.

To Lena's relief the limousine's telephone rang constantly on the journey out to the villa, engaging

Marcos's attention for most of the way. But she was aware, even as he talked business, of his eyes on her, their expression, when she inadvertently met them, curiously thoughtful.

If she read that expression right, he was only too willing to indulge in a little flirtatious lovemaking, even though he was now a married man. Maybe he even thought she'd be willing to have an affair with him. That was probably what he'd meant when he'd said he had something else in mind for her. Her conviction grew, and with it a sense of indignation. He'd planned to make her his mistress.

Only their arrival at the villa halted her racing thoughts.

Inside, Tassia Mavroleon took charge of Lena, greeting her kindly, though with some reserve, and Lena could hardly blame her. She felt that Marcos's escort placed her in an invidious position with his relations.

'Marianthe is not quite ready,' Tassia said, 'but you will find the other guests assembled in the salon.'

'It's very good of you to hold the dinner party here,' Lena said.

Tassia looked surprised.

'Why should I not? But please excuse me. I have some final orders to give to my staff.'

A little diffidently, Lena went into the salon. Expecting a large gathering commensurate with the size of the family, she was surprised to find so few of them present. The nun, Arietta, was there, as were Tassia's three sons— Christos being accompanied by a shy, pretty girl whom Lena took to be his fiancée. Apart from Marcos, that concluded the gathering.

Dimitri offered Lena a drink and asked, as he always did, after Chryssanti.

'In her last letter she was talking of going to college, to university even,' she told him. 'She's living with her grandparents at the moment. Her mother died, you know?'

'Yes, I am sorry. I wrote to Chryssanti, offering my condolences, but received no reply.' Obviously Dimitri was still *persona non grata* with his young cousin. It was as obvious that he deeply regretted it.

Lena looked around the sparsely populated room and found Marcos's frowning gaze on her and Dimitri. Hastily she looked away and forced an expression of animation in her face, as though Dimitri's society was all she wished for.

'I thought there would be more people here. Marianthe's parents at least; I know your grandfather's been ill.'

'*Ochi!*' It was a vehement negative accompanied by a backward jerk of his dark head, a click of his tongue.

'I suppose it wasn't convenient for them to come over to the mainland. The wedding would have been on Mykonos, of course?'

Against that strange denial which was so much more than a simple 'no.' Lena was puzzled.

'The wedding was a quiet one—in Athens,' Dimitri told her.

Lena thought she understood. Marianthe's escapade had blotted her copybook. She had been married off hastily to avoid any further rebellion, and was obviously still in everyone's bad books.

'I hope... Do you think she's...happy?' Is Marcos happy, is what you really want to know, she scolded herself.

'Ecstatically,' Dimitri said. 'They both are.'

She wanted Marcos to be happy, Lena told herself, of course she did, but it was hard to accept that he was finding that happiness with another woman.

'Which is more than they deserve,' Dimitri went on with rueful amusement, and she looked at him questioningly. But before she could query this strange remark there was a diversion as Marianthe, followed by Tassia, swept into the room, eyes sparkling, faces glowing.

'I'm so sorry to be late, everyone.' She saw Lena and came towards her, hands outstretched, a smile of friendly greeting on her lips. 'Lena! We have so much to talk about. I can't tell you how sorry I am for my churlish behaviour when we last met. I know now that you did the right thing. After dinner we must get together and I will tell you all about it, and how happy I am.'

Lena winced, and she was glad the younger girl had moved on and could not see the expression of pain she was sure must be in her eyes.

'The meal is ready to be served,' Tassia announced. 'Shall we go in?'

Dimitri came towards Lena and offered her his arm.

'As the eldest of the household,' he said gravely.

'*Signomi*, Dimitri, excuse me!' Marcos stepped between them. 'But Helena is *my* guest. The privilege is mine.'

'Marcos, no!' Lena was shocked to the core. 'You can't do this.'

'You would *prefer* to go in with *Dimitri*?' He sounded outraged.

'Yes, I would!' she snapped, and felt considerable satisfaction at his expression of annoyed chagrin. She turned to Dimitri, who was looking somewhat surprised, and slipped her hand through his arm.

'And my husband and I will lead the way,' Marianthe announced gaily. With a radiant smile, she took the arm of—*Manoli* Mavroleon!

'What is it, Lena?' Dimitri asked anxiously. 'You have gone quite pale. *Theos mou!* You are shaking. Are you ill?'

'No. Oh, please, Dimitri, don't draw attention to me. I'm all right—or I will be in a minute. I . . . I've just had a bit of a shock.' Leaning more heavily on his arm than she might have done, she let him lead her into the dining salon.

There was a moment of awkwardness when she found she was seated between Dimitri and Marcos, and a swift upward glance at Marcos showed the Black Lion very much in evidence. His normally sensuous lips were a straight line, his dark brows drawn together in an ominous frown.

'What was the shock?' Dimitri whispered in her ear as the first course was served.

An uneasy glance to her right showed Marcos being attentive to his other neighbour, Christos's fiancée. In a low voice she told Dimitri, 'I thought . . . I thought Marianthe was married to *Marcos*. The invitation just said Mr and Mrs *M* Mavroleon.'

There was a stunned silence. Then Dimitri gave a sudden shout of laughter which brought a pause in the conversation around the table and all eyes upon them.

'Sorry,' he muttered when the conversation level had returned to normal, 'but it struck me as very amusing. I see now why you gave poor Marcos his *congé*. It was not, after all, a preference for *my* company.'

'It sounds very rude,' Lena apologised. She picked nervously at her food. 'But that *was* the reason. You see, I thought Marcos was...' She gestured helplessly. It sounded too awful to tell.

'You thought that, although a newly married man, he was playing the *roué*.' Dimitri managed to stifle his chuckle this time. 'And what are you going to do about it?' he enquired interestedly.

'Do about it?' Any appetite she might have had destroyed, Lena was *distraite*. She pushed the unwanted food around her plate.

'Surely you will explain? He is obviously very displeased by what he sees as the transfer of your interest to me.'

Lena looked at him sharply.

'My interest?'

'Oh, come, Lena, some of us are not blind. Christos has seen it. I have seen it. My mother has seen it. You are in love with my cousin, *ne*? But Marcos, he does not know it, I think?'

Plates were whisked away by the highly efficient servants and replaced with the next course. Meanwhile Lena struggled to compose her thoughts. What a mess! How to extricate herself? But even if she straightened out the misunderstanding there was no guarantee that Marcos's feelings for her went any deeper than...than sexual desire. At the thought of it, and the manifestations he had displayed so many times, warmth rapidly suffused her. Haunted blue eyes met Dimitri's.

'What on earth am I going to do?'

'Take the first opportunity to explain,' Dimitri suggested. If only it were so easy.

'He may not *give* me an opportunity.'

Course followed course, and Lena knew she made a very poor pretence of eating. Fortunately her fellow guests were so immersed in their conversation that perhaps only the servants noticed the plates she returned almost untouched. For Lena conversation was desultory, since Dimitri had from time to time to pay attention to his left-hand neighbour, and Marcos did not once turn towards her.

Nevertheless she was tinglingly aware of him, of his body heat and strength. Once or twice his knee accidentally brushed hers, and once as she reached for a dish her hand made fleeting contact with his, adding to her torture. It was with heartfelt relief that she realised the meal was over and the ladies withdrawing.

'Lena, now we can talk!' Marianthe made a beeline for her, and for the next twenty minutes Lena was subjected to the younger girl's repeated apologies and explanations.

'My parents are still very angry with me—my mother less so than my father perhaps. But I think in time they will come round—especially,' she blushed charmingly, 'when there are grandchildren. But Marcos's grandfather! *Ochi!*' Her eyebrows raised expressively. 'I do not think he will forgive easily. The only thing I am sorry for,' she went on more soberly, 'is that in marrying my Manoli I must hurt Marcos. You will not know, perhaps, Lena, but Greek men are very proud, and we had been betrothed many years—all my life, in fact.'

'And . . . and he *was* hurt?' Lena enquired throatily.

'Oh, yes,' Marianthe said with disconcerting confidence. 'He would be, wouldn't he? But he was very kind. When he knew I did not want to marry him, that I wanted to marry his cousin, he said that of course he would release me from my promise. But it was not *my* promise, you understand, Lena,' Marianthe urged earnestly, 'it was made for me when I was born. I do not believe it was my fault that I could not keep it, do you?'

'Of course not,' Lena assured her. 'In your place, I'm sure I would have done the same.'

'He told my parents—I was afraid to do so. My father was very angry. At first he blamed Marcos. Apparently he thought it was *Marcos* who wished to be released from the engagement.' Marianthe laughed a little at the possibility.

The men rejoined the ladies, but did not circulate or make conversation with them. As Lena had seen at so many of the Theodopouloses' gatherings, the business the Mavroleons had discussed at table was carried into the drawing-room with them. The words 'shipping' and 'contracts' merged oddly with the ladies' talk of clothes and gossip about mutual friends.

As it grew later Lena began to think anxiously about the return journey to Athens. It was unlikely that Marcos would feel disposed to take her back, and yet, out of courtesy, he might consider himself obliged to do so. And everyone else was staying at the villa overnight.

'Helena!' The moment she was dreading had arrived. Marcos stood before her, his manner coldly formal, his expression glacial. 'It is time to leave.'

'I...I don't want to put you to any trouble,' she faltered.

'I have to return to Athens in any case.'

The round of farewells passed in a haze, and Lena felt faint with apprehension as she preceded Marcos into the back of the limousine.

The greater part of the journey passed in brooding silence. And yet there was a tension too, an awareness that lay between them. Finally, Lena nerved herself to say something. After all, the misapprehension and thus the offence had been hers. She swallowed.

'Marcos?'

In the gloom of the car she sensed the slight turn of his head. But he said nothing, gave her no help.

'Marcos, I'm *sorry*!'

No response

'Marcos,' she pleaded, 'this isn't easy for me. When I said I'd rather go into dinner with Dimitri...' She couldn't go on in the face of his continuing hostility.

'Yes?' It was encouragement of a kind, however grudging.

'When I said that, I thought you were married—to Marianthe.'

There was a sharp sound of indrawn breath.

'You were engaged to her,' Lena stumbled on. 'When she ran away you took her home. The invitation card said "Mr and Mrs *M* Mavroleon".' She broke off as her voice developed an ominous quiver.

With eyes squeezed tightly shut against the threatening tears, she felt his hand cover hers, imparting strength and warmth.

'I understand,' he said softly. 'I understand a great deal now. We have a lot to talk about, Helena, hmm?'

'H—have we?' she breathed uncertainly.

'Oh, yes.' He leaned forward and slid open the panel in order to give a few rapid instructions to his chauffeur. Then he settled back in his seat, but closer to Lena, his arm going about her.

After the trauma of the last few days it was bliss to relax against him without guilt, to bask in the solace of his embrace. As she nestled closer, she felt him draw in a deep breath.

'There's so much I want to say to you, Helena,' his voice was husky and he cleared his throat, 'that I scarcely know where to begin.' Her wrap had slipped aside and his fingers began to caress the smooth, bare skin of her shoulder.

She wished he would go on with whatever it was he wanted to say. Her stomach was knotted with tension again, due not only to this uncertainty but to his nearness. She breathed in the musky, masculine scent of him, and swallowed hard as she felt his hand move down to cup her breast. His fingers slipped beneath the soft, clinging material of her dress to tease a nipple already sensitised and hard. A delicious languor spread slowly through her. She wanted to be taken in his arms and kissed until her senses swam, and as though he divined her thoughts his free hand curved her throat and lifted her face, his lips lightly brushing hers.

It was not enough. She turned fully towards him, slipping her arms about his waist, holding on tight.

His kiss deepened as she had hoped it would, and her breasts rose and fell unevenly beneath his caressing hands. But he was aroused, too. He was trembling with passion, and she thrilled to the knowledge of her potent sexual influence upon him. His hands roamed freely over her now, stroking from waist to thigh, making her feel weak and languid. Her surroundings were quite forgotten, so that it came as a shock when Marcos put her gently away from him and she realised that the limousine had stopped outside Lydia's flat. A little regretful sigh shuddered through her as the chauffeur opened the door and she stepped out.

Marcos followed her and she looked up at him.

'Goodnight,' she murmured.

'Ah, not yet, *glyka mou*. Did you think I could leave you just like that? I am not made of stone.' The limousine was moving away and she looked questioningly at him. 'I told Spyros to go home. It would not be considerate to ask him to wait.' Insinuatively, 'I plan to be a long, long time.' Gently he urged her towards the building.

His words made shivers of delicious anticipation run through her. She didn't want him to leave yet. But if he stayed... And there was still too much unresolved.

'Marcos——' she said, her voice full of doubt.

His grasp tightened.

'I want to be alone with you, Helena. I do not think that Lydia will be back tonight. I want to make love to you a little longer.'

She wanted that, too. Marcos awakened in her a passion she'd never dreamed she was capable of. But she was afraid, too. She didn't want to lead him on, to start something she didn't intend to finish. It was too soon. She wasn't even sure what he wanted of her. Maybe not a long-term relationship. His marriage plans had been frustrated. *He* must be feeling frustrated. She didn't want to be used for meaningless sex.

They had reached the foyer and she had to make a decision now, before it was too late. Once she allowed him to accompany her upstairs, she had given tacit agreement to whatever he intended.

'Trust me, hmm?' he said softly. 'Nothing will happen that you don't *want* to happen.'

It was as well he could not read her body's throbbing message that gave him endless scope. It was a message he should not interpret.

'All right, you can come in, but not for long,' she warned him.

CHAPTER NINE

'I HAVE not been in Lydia's flat before.' Marcos looked around him appreciatively. 'But, as I would have expected, she has good taste.'

Lena wasn't sure whether she'd expected him to take her in his arms right away. But obviously he didn't intend to, and if he could be casual so could she.

'Would you like a coffee?' she asked.

'Thank you, yes.' He followed her into the kitchenette. 'I had not realised until recently that you were staying with Lydia. What happened to the apartment you were using?'

'It belonged to... to a friend. It wasn't convenient for me to stay there any longer. S—someone else was using it.'

'I wonder if I know this friend?' He was suddenly close behind her, so close that she could feel the warmth of his breath on her neck.

'Oh, I doubt it,' Lena said quickly.

With the percolator switched on, she had no further occupation until the coffee was ready, and she felt shy and awkward now that they were alone, with the barrier of Marcos's betrothal no longer between them. She wished she could think of something cool and sophisticated to say, some topic she could introduce that would fill this uneasy gap. But all she could think of was how very much she loved this man. All she could do was wonder just what it was he felt for her.

He seemed to sense her uncertainty, for he turned her towards him, his hands resting lightly on her shoulders. He gazed appraisingly into the cornflower-blue eyes.

'You are not afraid of me, *glyka mou*?' he asked gently.

She shook her head. It was true. She wasn't afraid of him. But she *was* afraid of being hurt.

'That is good.' His hands slipped down to her waist, her hips and finally to her buttocks. With a little groan he lifted her high against him, so that she was forced to put her arms about his neck to support herself. His lips brushed the curve of her neck, moved upwards to the sensitive place behind her ear and she turned her head, wanting his mouth on hers. He responded with little biting kisses, tormenting but unsatisfying, and she muttered a protest, her tongue coming out to flicker against his lips. She felt his chest rise in a long shudder, then his mouth closed over hers as she'd wanted it to, hungry, passionate, possessive, plundering deeper and deeper into its inviting warmth.

Lena could feel his body pounding with desire. They kissed and kissed, and passion throbbed and built within her.

She made a small sound in the back of her throat, wanting more. With a little grunt he released her, letting her slide the length of his body, letting her feel the evidence of his passion, a hard bulk between them. A flash of heat surged through her, but he was moving away from her, putting the width of the kitchenette between them.

'Not yet, Helena,' he said throatily, 'not yet. Let us get the talking over first, while I can still control myself. Surely that coffee must be ready now?'

She was swamped in a wave of disappointment and literal physical pain. But she knew he was right. They had to talk. She had to be sure of his motives. With hands that shook slightly, she poured coffee into two mugs and preceded him into the living-room. She sat down. She had to. Her legs felt weak and tremulous. But Marcos seemed unable to settle. He paced around the room sipping his coffee, stopping occasionally to inspect a book here, an ornament there, until Lena felt she could scream with the mounting tension. She sipped nervously at her coffee.

'You were surprised when you found Marianthe had married my cousin Manoli?' he said suddenly. It was a relief to have the silence broken. 'Yet you knew Marianthe did not want to marry *me*. She told me so. That is why you connived at her running away.'

'I knew she didn't want to marry you,' Lena confirmed, 'but I didn't think she had any choice. I thought her father would force her to go through with it.'

'He probably would have done,' Marcos said. 'But I refused to take an unwilling bride, to make a girl for whom I have a great deal of affection unhappy.'

'You...you said "affection".' Lena took a sip of her coffee to moisten her dry mouth. 'Weren't *you* in love with *her*, then?'

'No. But I could scarcely tell her that.'

Lena's heart thumped erratically.

'So what would have happened if she'd agreed to marry *you*?'

'If she had been in love with me, and since neither her father nor my grandfather would absolve me from the betrothal, I would have married her. It would have been a matter of honour.'

'But wouldn't that have made *you* unhappy?'

'Yes, but in this life we cannot always put our own happiness first.'

'But you did *want* to be released? You *asked* them?' Marcos grimaced.

'That was the cause of my argument with my grandfather on our last day at Skiapelos, the cause of a similar disagreement with Kyrios Lychnos when we returned Marianthe to Mykonos—*before* you helped her to run away.'

'And when you took her back again?'

'By then I knew she was not in love with me, that she preferred my cousin. That gave me a stronger lever against her father, at least.'

'And your grandfather?'

'He is still angry with me. He feels I should have insisted on the marriage taking place. When he found that Marianthe had married Manoli without his knowledge there was another quarrel, the one which led to his heart attack.'

'Do you think he'll ever forgive you?' Marcos was Thalassios's eldest grandson, the one in charge of his business affairs. 'Will he disinherit you?'

Marcos shrugged.

'As you know, my grandfather has a long memory. It took Irini's death for him to soften towards her. That was a little late.'

Lena dared not ask the question that obsessed her. Suppose Marcos wished to marry someone else. Would he feel constrained to get his grandfather's approval first? Her coffee was finished. She had no occupation for her hands. She clasped them tensely in her lap.

'And now, Helena,' Marcos too put down his empty mug, 'now that explanation is out of the way and with it—I hope—your scruples...' he stood before her, towering over her '...I can make love to *you*.'

But Lena was a little on guard now. He's said he didn't love Marianthe, but he hadn't even hinted that he might love *her*.

'Marcos, I don't think...'

'*Don't* think,' he urged her, 'allow yourself to *feel*—as you felt just a few moments ago. Then, you wanted me to make love to you.' He reached out for her and pulled her to her feet. 'I want to give you whatever you want, *glyka mou*.'

Then tell me you love me, she pleaded with him silently. She ached for him. Only tell me that and I'll do whatever you want me to do.

'Helena?' His voice was husky, sexily so. He put his arms around her, gently, unthreateningly, and with a little sigh she buried her face against his chest.

'Don't...don't rush me, Marcos,' she pleaded.

He misunderstood her fear.

'You shall have all the time in the world,' he assured her. He sat down and pulled her on to his knee. 'We will go at your pace. Kiss me, Helena,' he commanded. 'I want *you* to kiss *me*.'

The heat and strength of his body was working its old insidious spell, enveloping her in sensuality. But still she resisted him.

'I...I don't feel I really know you,' she prevaricated. It wasn't true. She knew all she wanted to know about this man, but for one thing. 'We haven't known each other very long.'

'It isn't time that matters, but the depth of feeling. And every time we are together there *is* that feeling between us. Kiss me, Helena,' he repeated. He captured her chin, forcing her to meet his gaze. As their eyes locked her pulses leaped and there was a delicious tightening in her abdomen. She cupped her hands around his jaw—blue-shadowed now and excitingly rough to her soft palms. She leaned forward slowly, saw the desire flare in his dark liquid eyes.

'All right,' she whispered as her mouth brushed his.

She had taken the initiative as he'd demanded, but that was all he allowed her. Now his mouth was in command and she wouldn't have wanted it any other way, Lena decided as she shifted and sighed, softening into his arms. His hands cupped her breasts and they tightened and swelled to his touch. Their nipples, taut and sensitive, strained against the soft material of her dress. He moved the balls of his thumbs against the hardened peaks, eliciting a fevered moan from her. He was so incredibly exciting.

'Do you want me, Helena?' Through the haze of passion his words reached her, making her limp and liquid with desire. 'Do you want me? Because I want you.' When she did not answer, his mouth began a fevered foray moving from her mouth to nibble at her neck, to trail along her jaw, over her cheeks, then back to her neck once more, moving down to where the 'V' of her neckline revealed the curve of her breasts and the shadowy cleft between. His caresses had an increased urgency, demanding primitive, ardent responses from her. 'Do you *want* me?' he repeated between kisses.

She trembled. Her head was spinning and she could not think clearly, but this was the moment of decision from which there would be no going back. The decision was taken.

'Yes, Marcos,' she whispered against his lips. 'Oh, yes, please!' Her hands moved over his back, but she wanted to feel his naked skin.

She unfastened his shirt and slid her hands beneath the silky material to feel the warmth of his bare skin. Her touch electrified him and without warning he stood, lifting her in his arms.

'Which is *your* room?' he demanded throatily.

At a nod of her head he carried her there and set her on her feet by the bed.

'How does this come off?' He inspected the buttons of her dress. Her own hands shaking, she helped him deal with them and the remainder of her clothes.

As she stood shyly before him, his eyes devoured her naked loveliness.

'*Kalliste!* Most beautiful!' He breathed as he cupped her breasts. He lowered his head to take one aching nipple in his mouth, and sharp as an arrow she felt sensation deep within the feminine core of her.

She wanted him to take his clothes off too, and her fingers worked on the buttons of his shirt; as he made a wordless sound of pleasure, she felt for the zipper of his trousers.

'Gently, Helena, slowly,' he murmured. 'We have waited a long time for this. We will make it a memorable occasion.' Again he kissed her tingling breasts, circling the tip of each nipple with his tongue.

She was nearly out of her mind with need. She plunged her hands into the thick blue-black hair at the nape of his neck, pulling his head up so that she could kiss him; long, slow, voluptuous kisses.

His hand slid over her stomach, slowly, oh, so slowly, before it moved lower. Lena sucked in her breath. She wanted him to touch her more intimately. Go on, she urged him silently, go on. His fingers moved further, and she blushed as she could not disguise her reactions. She couldn't breathe, couldn't speak.

'Marcos, please,' she begged, wanting him to stop this delicious torment and make love to her fully.

'In a moment, *agape mou*. Be patient. Enjoy.' He whispered erotic endearments against her mouth as he caressed her until she felt she would explode with the tensions that mounted inside her.

'Very soon, my love, very soon,' he told her, and now he allowed her urgent hands to reach for him.

A shrill sound cut across the moment. For a moment Lena couldn't think what it was, then she groaned.

'The doorbell!'

'Ignore it! Leave it!' Marcos commanded, holding her tightly against him.

'I can't. We can't.'

'We can,' he insisted. 'Whoever it is will go away.'

'But they'll be able to see the lights. And it might be Lydia. I . . .'

He swore expressively and began to refasten his trousers.

'Then stay there. Don't move. I'll go.'

Still shuddering, aching for his return, she sat on the edge of the bed, listening.

The voices in the hall were both male. Hurriedly, Lena pulled on her dressing-gown and went out into the living-room. Marcos entered first and she saw at once that he was furiously angry. His face was drawn into a scowl, and behind him came a familiar figure.

'Petros!' But, before she could demand the reason for her ex-fiancé's presence, Marcos spoke.

'Since you have another visitor, one who claims a prior right, *our business*,' he edged the words with satire, 'will have to wait. I'll see you in my office first thing Monday morning. Don't be late.' And he was gone, slamming the door behind him.

'So *that* was the Black Lion of Skiapelos,' Petros commented. 'An apt title. And what was *he* doing here— and you dressed like that? You objected to my presence in similar circumstances. Only then *you* weren't the one who was half-naked, as you are now.' And Lena realised that her robe had loosened, exposing the deep cleft between her bare breasts. Hastily she adjusted it.

'Why are you here?' Lena demanded. 'How did you find me?' She felt totally drained. Petros couldn't have timed his arrival for a more inopportune moment.

'Simple. I merely asked the chauffeur you sent round for your luggage where he was taking it. I must say *he* seemed a little disconcerted by his surroundings. I suppose you didn't happen to tell Mavroleon whose apartment you were using?'

'No. Your uncle particularly asked me not to mention his name.'

'Yes, he would.' Petros sounded amused.

This was an opportunity to find out just what was the cause of the enmity between Domenicos Theodopoulos and Thalassios Mavroleon, but Lena didn't take it. She was too anxious to be rid of her uninvited visitor.

'What do you want, Petros?'

'A little information.'

'Information?' She was puzzled. 'What about?'

'Sit down, Lena.' He pointed to a chair. 'We may as well be comfortable.'

'You're not staying long enough to get comfortable. I want you out of here. My flatmate will be home soon,' she lied. Nevertheless, she sat down. Her legs still felt shaky from Marcos's lovemaking. She felt hollow and bereft. She could kill Petros for this interruption. 'What did Marcos mean when he said you had a prior right to visit me?'

'I told him I was your fiancé. But never mind that,' he said impatiently as she gave a gasp of horror and outrage, 'what I want to know...'

'You *what*? Oh, how dare you? You had no right to tell him that.'

Petros grinned maliciously.

'Queered your pitch with him, have I? Did you think you'd found yourself a substitute husband, Lena—and a multi-millionaire to boot?'

'No,' she said with quiet scorn. 'No, I didn't think that.' Then, in renewed alarm, 'You didn't give him your *full* name?'

'No.'

'Thank God for that.' She was still angry at the lie he'd told. But, now she thought about it, he might not have done her a disservice. Able to think more rationally now Marcos was no longer near her, she realised she might have been about to do something incredibly foolish. He'd made no commitment to her, no promises.

'You asked me what I want,' Petros cut across her thoughts, 'and I said information. I want you to tell me what you know about this American deal the Mavroleons are involved in—facts and figures.'

She gasped at his audacity.

'No way!' Then, 'How do *you* know anything about America?'

Petros smiled smugly.

'Rumours, just rumours at first. Everyone in our circle knew there was something in the wind and that it was the kind of thing to interest the Mavroleons. So when I discovered you were working for them...'

'You thought you'd come here and do a little industrial espionage.' Lena's expression as she looked at the man she'd once thought she loved was full of contempt. 'You're despicable,' she told him.

'Oh, but you're the one who's going to do the "espionage", as you call it.'

Lena gave a disbelieving laugh.

'You're out of your mind if you think I'd tell *you* anything.'

'But you've already been extremely helpful, my dear Lena.' She stared at him uncomprehendingly. 'So thoughtful of you to give me access to your briefcase the other night. I spent several most instructive hours reading through the contents.'

Lena felt as though her face must have gone chalk-white. Her facial skin seemed too tight and her lips quivered, but with anger now.

'So you see, Lena, I already know a considerable amount about the deal with America. And since my father-in-law...' He stopped and bit his lip, a look of chagrin crossing his face, but Lena pounced on the slip.

'Your father-in-law! Who just happens to be a Texas oil millionaire, you were going to say? So you're married! And you had the insufferable gall to give me all that rubbish about realising your mistake, wanting me back.'

'Disappointed, Lena?' he jeered.

'Yes!' she flashed. 'I am, but not for myself. I'm disappointed in you. When you threw me over, I thought at least your expressions of regret were genuine. I'd persuaded myself you couldn't help what happened. But I realise now I didn't really know you at all, Petros Theodopoulos. You're a scheming, unscrupulous... I shall write to your uncle and tell him what you're like.'

Petros burst into loud, rude laughter.

'When it comes to doing the Mavroleons out of a big deal, I know whose side he'd be on.'

'Come off it,' Lena said. 'I know he fell out with old Thalassios years ago, but I can't believe...'

'Believe it, Lena,' Petros said more soberly, and with a conviction that chilled her. 'You don't think Domenicos helped Irini Mavroleon just out of the goodness of his heart, do you?'

'He insisted that his name shouldn't be mentioned.'

'Only because Irini was also Domenicos's niece.'

'What?'

'You mean to say you didn't know? Old Thalassios Mavroleon was married three times. His second wife was Domenicos's sister, Tina. It was an arranged marriage, like the first one. The two families were the best of friends. But then a few years later he divorced Tina to marry his third wife, Rallia. Since then Thalassios and Domenicos have been at daggers drawn. Anything one could do to spike the other's guns, they did. That's why the Mavroleons don't have an office in London. Domenicos told the British Authorities that Thalassios was involved in some sharp practice, had him made *persona non grata*. So you see, Lena, you're going to give me the information I want. Otherwise I'm really going to spoil things for you with Mavroleon. You see, my dear, the very indiscreet Sally has told me about your letters. She doesn't like me, and she took great delight in telling me you'd fallen in love with someone else. She also told me who you were working for, and I put two and two together. One word from me—about how you used to work for my uncle—and there's no way the Mavroleons will believe you weren't spying for us.'

She'd been foolish and careless, and the dupe of two unscrupulous men—even though she found it incredible that Domenicos, of all people, should use her like this. He had always been a kind and considerate employer.

But to add more to the information she'd unwittingly given away wouldn't improve things. No, there was no way she was going to allow herself to be blackmailed. To give in to it was not the answer. Who was it who had said 'publish and be damned!'? Despite her personal despair, there was a savage satisfaction in defying Petros. And perhaps, just perhaps, she could call his bluff. Perhaps, when Petros realised his threat was unavailing, he'd decide not to carry it out.

'You can tell him whatever you like,' she said. 'In fact, I hope you do. At least he'll know what and who he's up against. But you're getting no secrets out of me.'

But ten minutes later, after Petros too had slammed out of the apartment, she wept bitterly. She didn't know whether she had Marcos's love, but at least until now she'd had his trust. Despite what she'd told Petros, she didn't like the idea that Marcos's faith in her integrity would be destroyed. And then, with a sinking heart, Lena realised that even if Petros didn't carry out his threat, she couldn't leave it at that. The Theodopouloses were already in possession of information that might be damaging to Marcos's dealings with the Americans. She had no choice. She had to tell Marcos the truth about Petros and the dangerous knowledge he had obtained.

She hadn't felt like this on a Monday morning since she'd been a child and forgotten to do her homework. The sick apprehension was with her from the moment she woke up, and by the time she reached the offices of the Mavroleon corporation and stepped into the lift she was cold with fear, despite another warm Athens morning.

As she entered the sixth-floor office she shared with Lydia, the other girl gave her a worried look.

'Marcos wants to see you, the minute you get in. He looks really furious about something.'

So Marcos's anger hadn't abated since Saturday night, and when he'd heard what she had to tell him he would be even angrier. Her heart in her boots, she knocked on the office door.

To her surprise Marcos wasn't alone. Ranged around the office were his three cousins, their faces all as grim as his. All? No, one perhaps held a glint of sympathy. Dimitri was looking at her as if he felt sorry for her. The usually courteous Marcos did not even ask her to sit down, and it was Dimitri again who offered her one of the deep leather chairs.

Marcos did not waste time on a preamble.

'Dimitri came back yesterday from America. He went there hoping to return with a signed contract. He found instead that our confidentiality had been breached. Understandably the Americans are annoyed. There is some doubt now whether they will do business with us.'

'Marcos——' In the white oval of her face her cornflower-blue eyes pleaded with him for a hearing. 'Marcos, I...'

'That confidentiality was breached from *this* office. Since yesterday I have been making enquiries. I now know how and why. Helena!' he rapped out her name. 'Is your fiancé still in Athens?'

'He's not...' she began, but she was not allowed to continue.

'He has left you again so soon? But of course he has obtained what he came here to find out. I am only surprised you did not go with him and make your escape while you could. But perhaps you hoped to do some more spying?'

'No!' she cried indignantly. 'I...'

'I should have suspected something. You were always very outspoken in your views about Greeks and their ways. And then you picked up our office routines with an ease that should have made me suspicious. When you spoke of a broken romance, I believed you.' Marcos's deep voice was heavy with self-disgust. 'Now I discover you are still engaged, that your fiancé is a Greek, one of a family very well known to us. You worked for them in London?' It was phrased as a question. But he *knew*.

'Yes...I...But Marcos, he's not...I'm not...I didn't...'

'When you first came here, you were living with him in his apartment.'

'I was there *alone*,' she said fiercely.

'Then he joined you later,' Marcos's tone was impatient. 'Let us not quibble. The fact remains that you were staying there and Spyros saw him when he collected your luggage. The only thing that puzzles me is why you moved in with Lydia. That I do not understand at all.'

'No, you wouldn't,' Lena said bitterly. 'You're so determined to condemn me. All of you.' She looked around at the grim faces. 'You're very ready to believe I could be guilty of such disloyalty.'

'Lena.' It was Dimitri who spoke, gently, regretfully. 'It is well known that one cannot serve two masters. In this case, obviously, your loyalty was to Domenicos Theodopoulos and to your fiancé.'

'No, no, *no*! You don't understand! Any of you.' She was almost sobbing now, yet pride would not let the tears fall. If only she'd been alone with Marcos she might have been able to get through to him, to convince him. She might even have told him that she loved him, that she would never have betrayed his trust. But she wouldn't beg and plead in front of all these stony-faced men.

Perhaps that was why Marcos had lined them all up to face her. The thought that he might have been afraid of weakening gave her hope. 'I'd like to speak to you alone,' she told him.

'*Kolasiz!*' He swore. 'Never! You will see Lydia, collect your pay and be out of this building in the next half-hour. I do not wish to see you again—ever!'

Lena managed to hold herself together until she reached the outer office, then, to Lydia's consternation, she collapsed weeping into a chair. For a few moments she was too incoherent to answer the older girl's anxious questions. Then the story poured out of her, haphazardly, lacking chronological order. But at last Lydia was in possession of all the facts.

'And it's not true, Lydia. I would never, never have abused my position here. I'm *not* engaged to Petros. I haven't been since I left England. He's married, for heaven's sake—to an American girl. That's why he's so interested in the American contract.'

'Didn't you tell Marcos all this?'

'He wouldn't let me get a word in edgeways. Every time I tried to defend myself he just cut across me in a cold, horrible way. I didn't know he could be so...so...'

'He is one of the Black Lions of Skiapelos,' Lydia said simply. 'When they are hurt, they roar. He is all the more hurt because he is in love with you.'

'In love with me? *Me?*' Lena gave a cynical laugh that became a strangled sob. 'You're joking!'

Lydia shook her head.

'I have known it for a long time. That is why I said the other secretaries here were jealous, that they did not stand a chance—now.'

'I thought you meant because he was engaged to Marianthe. Anyway, I still don't believe it. If he loved me, he couldn't think this of me. If you love someone, you trust them.' She stood up. 'I'd better go.'

'But you can't just leave like this. There are wages owing to you.'

'I wouldn't touch another penny of his money,' Lena said wearily. 'I don't need it, do I?' she enquired sarcastically. 'My *fiancé* has just filched a big deal from under Marcos's nose.'

'So you admit it!'

With a little gasp, Lena swung round to see Marcos in the doorway, his cousins ranged behind him, and now even Dimitri was looking at her accusingly.

'No,' she said desperately. 'I didn't mean it like that. I...'

'Get out!' The thrust of his square-cut jaw was belligerent and he pointed a finger towards the door in a gesture that ought to have been ridiculously dramatic, but wasn't. 'Get out of my sight!'

CHAPTER TEN

'I AM coming back to the apartment with you,' Lydia told Lena defiantly, as Marcos made a protesting sound. 'She is in no fit state to go wandering through Athens on her own.'

'I don't want you to get into trouble with Marcos on my account,' Lena protested as they went down in the lift, the older girl's arm about her shoulders.

'I shall not be dismissed, if that is what worries you,' Lydia told her confidently. 'Right at this moment Marcos cannot do without me. You won't really give up and go home, will you?' she asked in the taxi taking them to the apartment. 'You are innocent. Why not stay and prove it?'

'So *you* believe me?' Lena said gratefully.

'Yes, and so should Marcos, only his judgement is clouded by jealousy of the man he believes to be your fiancé. The truth *will* come out, Lena. I am sure of it. Stay in Athens and give Marcos a chance to find out, to make amends.'

Wearily, Lena shook her head.

'I've no way of proving it. Petros has told his lies too well. I just want to get away and put the whole miserable business behind me. I'm going back to England on the first plane I can get.'

It was easier said than done. A strike at all Greek airports had every aeroplane grounded for an indefinite period.

172

'Everything's conspiring against me,' Lena said despairingly. But Lydia disagreed.

'I believe the gods are on your side. They are keeping you here for a reason. And you know you are very welcome to stay on at my apartment for as long as you like.'

For several days Lena did just that. She stayed within the same four walls with no heart to go out into the city she had come to love, not just for its own sake, but for its associations with the man she loved even more. Each day when Lydia returned from the office Lena looked at her questioningly, hoping against hope that there would be some news of Marcos relenting. But every day Lydia shook her head.

'He never mentions your name, though I have been honest with him. I have told him you are still in Athens. He is not happy either,' she went on. 'The Black Lion is very much in evidence. No one is safe from his temper and his tongue.'

When news came at last that the airport strike had been broken, Lena booked the first available flight.

'In two days' time I'll be back in London,' she told Lydia sadly, 'and all this will seem like a dream—a bad one.' Her packing was done. All she had to do was wait.

She spent her last day sitting out on the balcony. She might as well make the most of the sun, she told herself grimly. There would be little enough in England, with autumn approaching and winter close behind. She tried to read to keep her mind off the fact that tomorrow she would be putting so many miles between her and Marcos, but she could not concentrate. Her thoughts ranged over all the places they had seen together, and particularly the Acropolis in its varying moods. She would never again be able to look at a picture of those noble ruins

without remembering Marcos and all that he meant to
her. Perhaps she would make one last pilgrimage there
before she left Greece forever. It was unlikely she would
ever feel detached enough to return.

Lost in these unhappy thoughts, she started violently
when the doorbell sounded. No matter how many times
it had rung in the last few days, there had always been
the slim chance that it might be Marcos come in search
of her, his doubts of her somehow dispelled. And as
always she hurried to answer it.

'Domenicos!' She ought to have shut the door in his
face, but old habits of courtesy died hard, and he took
advantage of her slight recoil to step inside.

'Helena!' he said, his deeply lined face grave.

She recovered herself. 'You've got a damned nerve,
coming here like this, after all the trouble you and Petros
have caused me.'

'That is exactly why I *am* here,' Domenicos told her.
'To try and put things right. I insisted that Petros give
me your address, and I beg you to give me a fair hearing,
Helena.'

That was what she'd hoped for from Marcos. And
perhaps if he'd granted it things might have been very
different now. Wanting justice for herself, she could give
no less to Domenicos.

'All right,' she said flatly, 'I'll hear you out. But it'd
better be good.'

She led the way into the living-room and sat down.

'Firstly,' Domenicos said, 'I would like to assure you
I played no part in Petros's actions while he was in
Athens.' Lena's look told him 'pull the other one', and
he went on hastily, 'The only deception I practised was
in not revealing my relationship to Irini—that she was
my niece. But I did not feel it was necessary, and we had

decided her children should not be told at that time. And I certainly could not know how closely *you* would become connected with the Mavroleons. What *is* your present position with them?'

'I don't have one,' Lena said bitterly. 'I've been sacked. Thanks to your nephew, they think I've been stealing commercial secrets, to pass on to *your* firm.'

'I had the impression that there was more—between you and one of Thalassios's grandsons? Sally certainly seemed to think so.'

'There might have been something,' Lena said flatly. 'I'm not sure what. But whatever it was is finished.'

'I am sorry.' His regret certainly *sounded* genuine.

'Petros claims you sent him to Athens specifically to find out what deals the Mavroleons were involved in— particularly the American one.'

'Yes,' Domenicos agreed, 'I sent him. Business is still business and the Mavroleons still my rivals.' As Lena drew an indignant breath, he held up his hand. 'But he had no instructions to make use of *you*, or to blacken your name. I beg you to believe that, Helena. I have always had a great affection for you, and you know how sorry I was to lose your services. Even more so not to be able to welcome you into my family.'

'Yes.' That was true, and Lena felt herself softening towards the old man.

'I am seriously displeased with Petros. In fact, if he were not my heir I should be inclined to dismiss him. As it is...' he shrugged philosophically '...there is no one else. Stephen will no doubt become a Mavroleon in all but name.'

'There's Chrys. You know she's back in England?'

'Yes. But I cannot leave my firm to a woman.' Again he silenced Lena's protest. 'It is not the tradition of my family. But Chryssanti has accepted my offer of help. With her English grandparents' consent, I am putting her through university.' He hesitated, then, 'Since I am in Athens, I hear a rumour that my old friend Thalassios is unwell. How did *you* find him?'

'When I first met him he was very well. But since then he's had a heart attack.'

'Is it serious?'

'Serious enough, I believe.'

'Hmm.' Domenicos looked thoughtful. 'I might just go and see Thalassios, if they will let me anywhere near him.' And, at Lena's look of surprise, 'I feel I should like to make my peace with my friend. We are both growing older and age brings better counsel. The apostle Paul wrote that one should never allow the sun to set on one's wrath. I do not argue with his philosophy, and I find I do not wish the sun of life to go down on our anger. My sister,' he added with apparent inconsequentiality, 'still loves the old fool.'

Lena asked the question that had been vexing her ever since she'd discovered Domenicos's relation by marriage to the Mavroleons.

'Why, if the Mavroleons were still your enemies—and you were still trying to do them down in business, why on earth did you *want* to send Irini's children to them?'

Domenicos sighed heavily.

'As I told you, business is still business—friend *or* enemy. With regard to Irini, I admit I could not altogether approve of her wish to send her children to her father. But,' he crossed himself, 'who dares deny the wishes of a dying woman—my only sister's daughter?'

'What brings you to Athens, then?' Lena asked him. 'Surely you're not just here to see me?'

'No. I had to come on business.' He grinned lop-sidedly. 'And the less you know about that the better. But when Petros boasted to me of the way he'd used your position with the Mavroleons and that he'd probably ruined your new romance too, I had an added incentive.'

'Well, I *do* appreciate your coming to see me,' Lena told him. 'But,' she sighed as Domenicos rose to take his leave of her, 'I'm afraid it can't undo the harm that's been done. I'm going back to England tomorrow.'

'When I return to London, perhaps you would like to come and see me about a job?' Domenicos suggested.

'And work under the same roof as Petros again? No way!'

When Lydia returned from work that evening she found Lena in a strange mood. Lena had prepared a meal for both of them, but was unable to eat her own share.

'I'm going out,' she announced suddenly after they had cleared away and stacked the crockery in the dishwasher.

'Where?' Lydia asked, then, 'I am sorry. I have no right to question your comings and goings. But I am concerned for you.'

'I'll be all right,' Lena assured her. 'One thing I've discovered about Greece is that I never need to feel nervous being out alone—even at night. I just want to see the Acropolis one more time. It . . .' she flushed be-trayingly, 'it's a rather special place for me.'

'I understand,' Lydia said gently. 'But do not be too unhappy, Lena. I feel that the gods will bring you back to Greece some day. They have always smiled on true love.'

*　　*　　*

Like a big oval island, the Acropolis floated above the sea of roofs that was the city of Athens. Floodlights played not only on its columns but on its cliffs, disguising the depredations of years and weather and making it seem a fitting dwelling for the gods. Lena climbed up the steep slope that gave access to the almost level plateau on which the temples stood.

She made her way to the centre of the plateau. Before her lay the Parthenon with its rows of marble columns—defaced, but still things to be marvelled at. There was an atmosphere up here at night, alone, which could not be captured at any other time. Lena had the sense of being in her own private chapel. But it was not without a wry smile at her own superstitious behaviour that she closed her eyes and offered up a prayer—not to the Christian god she and her family had always worshipped, but to Pallas Athene, the patron of Athens.

She felt no sense of being heard or answered, but then she had expected none. But she did feel calmer and more resigned to tomorrow's departure. Perhaps her obsession with Marcos had been a madness brought about by the romance of Greece, the enervating effect of its glaring sun. Perhaps at home she would recover her sanity. She sat down at the foot of a broken column and rested her back against it and stared out over the city. It was chilly up here, and the marble against which she leaned was cold, but it didn't seem to matter. It was in keeping with the ice that encased her heart.

Time passed but still she sat on, unwilling to take her leave of this now doubly sacred spot. Afterwards she thought she might have dozed a little, for undoubtedly she was dreaming that Marcos was speaking to her.

'Helena! Thank God I have found you. Lydia thought you might be here, but you have been gone so long.'

Still in a daze she opened her eyes to see him crouching before her, the floodlights illuminating his craggy features, in which his eyes were deep and unfathomable.

'Marcos?' Her brain felt numb, incapable of rational thought. She still couldn't believe he was here.

'Yes, *glyka mou*.' His voice was unbelievably tender. She hadn't thought to hear him call her that again. 'Come.' He put a hand on her arm. '*Christos*, but you are cold. And stiff,' he said as he pulled her to her feet. With his arm about her, he began to lead her back down the slope.

'Where are you taking me? Why are you here?' Her state of calm euphoria banished by his arrival, her chilled body had begun to tremble. Her eyes pricked with tears. 'I thought I'd never see you again.'

'And if it had been left to me, stiff-necked fool that I am, you might never have done so. We Greeks do not find it easy to admit we are wrong, but ah, Helena, can you ever forgive me for doubting you?'

She could forgive *him* anything, she thought, if only he would tell her that he loved her. Her cold feet stumbled a little over the last stretch of ground, and with a muffled curse he swung her up into his arms and carried her the remaining few yards to where his limousine stood, its engine running.

Spyros did not wait for instructions. The moment Marcos had lowered his precious burden into the rear of the vehicle, it glided away.

Wrapped in Marcos's arms, Lena could still not believe what was happening to her.

'Where are we going?' she asked again.

'Where I should have taken you a long time ago,' he muttered.

It was only a short drive to Marcos's town house. Lena recognised the street at once. Still shivering, she allowed him to help her up the steps and into the building.

Inside they were met by the same elderly, stern-faced woman she had seen on her only other visit to Marcos's home. At the old woman's severe expression, Lena, who felt strangely light-headed now, began to giggle weakly.

'She doesn't approve of me at all, does she? She probably thinks I'm drunk.'

'It is not *her* place to disapprove of *you*,' Marcos said. 'And in future no one shall disapprove of you. No one!' He rapped out a few peremptory orders in his own tongue, and with a startled exclamation the housekeeper bustled away. 'I have told her to bring some warm soup. You are chilled to the bone and Lydia tells me you ate nothing before you went out. Are you trying to make yourself ill?' he scolded. He settled her in a chair and knelt before her, chafing her hands between his.

For the moment Lena was content to lean back and submit unquestioningly to his ministrations. It was enough that she was here with him, whatever it might mean.

The housekeeper was back in record time with the soup. As it began to warm her inside, as Marcos's touch had warmed her exterior, Lena's numbed brain began to function again.

'Why did you come and look for me?' she asked.

'Because I discovered I had done you a great wrong—that you were not a spy for the Theodopouloses. I went to Lydia's first, hoping against hope to find you still there. *Christos!* Another day and I would have missed you. But I would have followed you to England, Helena *mou*, believe me.'

'How did you find out?'

'I had a visitor today—a most unexpected one,' he said grimly. 'A man I would not have expected to dare to cross our threshold—Domenicos Theodopoulos himself.'

'*He* told you?'

'Yes. Had he been on his own, I probably would not have believed him any more than I believed you. But, Helena, he brought my *grandfather* with him, to re-inforce his argument. Those two cussed old men have made up a quarrel of some thirty years' standing. Would you credit it?'

'Oh, I *am* glad!' Lena exclaimed. Then, with concern, 'But your grandfather—was he really well enough to travel?'

'He seemed to have shed years,' Marcos told her. 'Oh, our two families will probably always remain business rivals. A Greek businessman is always a businessman.'

'But it will be a *friendly* rivalry,' Lena said happily.

'Hmn, maybe!' Marcos said with a wry smile. Then once more his features were severe. 'But there will be no question of a truce with *Petros* Theodopoulos.'

Lena had long since finished her soup. She set down the bowl and looked at Marcos uncertainly. Where did they go from here? He, it seemed, had ideas about that.

'And now,' he told her, 'you are going to bed.'

'You're going to take me back to Lydia's apartment?' It was difficult to keep the disappointment out of her voice.

'No. I gave my housekeeper instructions to prepare a bed here for you.' He seemed to be watching her re-action closely.

'Isn't that a bit...a bit...unconventional?'

'Maybe,' he said with a certain grimness, 'but I am beginning to believe that some traditions are best disposed of. Come.' He held out his hand. 'I will show you the way.'

Lena had never been upstairs in Marcos's house, and she felt well enough now to look about her in silent wonder as they mounted the semicircular staircase built against one wall. Vibrant, glowing Old Masters lined the wall and that of the wide landing above. The room to which he showed her was richly furnished with sumptuous pile carpets, brocaded fabrics and the most enormous double bed she had ever seen. The sight of the bed made her realise just how weary she was. It looked so inviting, a bed into which one might sink and be almost lost.

'There must be room for six in that,' she commented. Her spirits had undergone an enormous uplift, and though to her the future still seemed uncertain her sense of humour was returning.

'I think *I* would settle for two,' Marcos said. His voice was suddenly throaty and, startled, she turned to took at him. He had closed the door behind them and there was an expression on his face that she recognised only too well. It was dark with passion, his eyes glittering. She flushed scarlet as her pulses leapt in response.

'M...Marcos,' she croaked. She cleared her throat and tried again. 'Marcos, you don't mean...you... we...?'

'Oh, but I do, *agape mou*.' He stared into her widened blue eyes and she moistened her lips with her tongue. 'Finally we're alone together with no obstacles, no misunderstandings between us.'

There was one little area of doubt that had not been cleared up, but she was in love with him, and for now nothing seemed more important than that, she thought as he pulled her close, then closer. And she did not protest as his mouth came down fiercely on hers. It seemed a lifetime since he had last kissed her.

The days apart, the longing for him that had seemed so futile, had primed her body for his touch, and his kiss was like that of a starving man: hot, hard and deep.

She lifted her arms as he pulled her cotton T-shirt up. 'Foolish one, to go out at night dressed only in this,' he scolded tenderly. But then his attention was given to her breasts as he cupped and kissed them.

She moaned breathlessly and arched under his hands. 'Undress me,' he murmured, and she fumbled with the buttons of his shirt, feverish in her actions until she could tangle her fingers in the wiry dark hair on his chest.

She was dizzy and trembling at the sweet sensations his lips and hands were arousing. She wound her arms around his neck, making wild little sounds in her throat.

His hand had reached the waistband of her jeans now, and the fastening gave easily to his importuning and she moaned at the new intense pleasures he was giving her.

He was whispering in his own tongue, and yet his words sounded incredibly sexy. Only as he began to ease her jeans down over her buttocks did she hesitate, holding back a little.

'Do not be afraid of me, Helena.' He completed the removal of the garment, his touch as he did so a long, sensual caress. Somehow, while retaining his hold on her, he managed to shed his own clothes, then pulled her once more against his powerful nude body. It was obvious how much he wanted her.

Gently he pressed her down on to the bed, moving swiftly to cover her, parting her thighs with his.

She knew a moment's fear before he moved into her, linking their bodies together. But then she knew that whatever the outcome might be she wanted to give him everything: body, soul, heart and mind. She couldn't hold back. She loved him far too much. Slowly, sensuously, he aroused her until her breath came irregularly and within her there was a turmoil so intense she could only cling to Marcos while a violent explosion of sensation rocked her, rocked them both into a new dimension of experience.

Afterwards, as they lay still entwined, sated by their passion, Lena replayed their lovemaking in her mind. It had been as wonderful—more wonderful than she had dreamt it would be. But was it possible those shattering moments could ever be repeated? Fear gripped her. Suppose this was all Marcos had wanted of her? He had spoken of breaking with traditions, but that might not necessarily include those of marriage.

Even as Marcos's arms tightened about her, she told herself she mustn't allow herself to be lulled into a false sense of security. She'd had those few moments. She must be prepared to settle for that and no more. It was a richer memory than she had expected to take home with her. On that thought, incredibly, she fell asleep.

She woke late to find herself alone. There was no sign of Marcos, no evidence that he had ever shared this room. His clothes were gone and hers lay in a neat pile on a chair. She wondered who had tidied up, and flushed with embarrassment at the thought that it might have been the grim-faced housekeeper.

There was a gentle knock on the bedroom door, and a maidservant peeped in.

'Ah, you are awake, *thespinis*.' She came further into the room. 'Kyrios Marcos thought you might like your breakfast in bed.' She deposited the tray she carried across Lena's knees. 'He asks if you can be ready to leave in half an hour?' And at Lena's affirmative the maid withdrew.

Lena supposed Marcos would be taking her back to Lydia's flat. But what then? Was it to be goodbye? Perhaps Marcos thought last night had made amends for his suspicions of her. She shuddered. She had wanted him so much, and after thinking she would never see him again she had been acutely vulnerable, unable to refuse the passion that had swept them into bed together. She knew with a shaming certainty that he would not have treated a woman of his own race in that way, outside of marriage. No Greek girl would have *behaved* that way. In sudden self-revulsion, she pushed her breakfast away untasted.

When the little maid came to remove the tray, she carried two suitcases. She looked disapprovingly at the untouched food, but made no comment.

'Kyrios Marcos has collected your other clothes from Thespinis Lydia's apartment. He asks that you wear a dress this morning.'

Lena considered ignoring this suggestion. She felt a niggling irritation that she knew really stemmed from an uneasy conscience. She had always had strong moral views, feeling that the deeper intimacies between man and woman should be kept for marriage. She despised herself for lowering her standards, and felt Marcos could hardly be blamed for despising her too.

However, she did put on a dress, a white Greek cotton she had purchased but never worn, and matched it with high-heeled strappy sandals. Anxiously she considered her face in the mirror, but apart from the shadowed uncertainty in her eyes it showed no signs of last night's earth-shattering experience.

She had to take several deep, steadying breaths before she emerged from her room and went downstairs to face Marcos. What would she see in *his* eyes?

He was waiting for her in the entrance hall and greeted her with a smile and every appearance of normality.

'Sh...should I have brought my suitcases down with me?' Perhaps he was planning to take her to the airport himself.

'No.' A hand under her elbow, he ushered her outside to where his limousine, with Spyros at the wheel, awaited them.

'Where are we going?'

'How do you feel about a Greek wedding?'

Lena had a sense of *déjà vu*. But she'd been misled by those words once before.

'Who's getting married this time?'

His answer electrified her.

'We are.'

'But you haven't *asked* me to marry you.' Blue eyes wide, she stared at him in disbelief.

He put a hand under her chin and regarded her severely.

'What do you think last night was all about, *agape mou*?'

'I was beginning to wonder,' she confessed. But, cautiously, joy was beginning to expand within her.

'You did not think I would take you to my bed if I did not intend to marry you?' He sounded quite shocked. 'I told you, Helena *mou*, we Greeks respect and cherish our women.'

'But you never said anything about...about *love*,' she reminded him.

He made a little sound, a throaty rumble in his throat, and his eyes darkened in a way she recognised.

'Everything I did to you last night—every caress, every kiss told you of my love. But if you would have it in words, *glyka mou*...' He pulled her into his arms, and his lips against hers he murmured over and over again, '*S'agapo*, Helena, I love you. Will you marry me?'

'B...but your family—your grandfather...'

'I have told my grandfather that unless I marry you I shall *never* marry.' A smile lit Marcos's dark eyes and his words made Lena blush. 'The thought that he might be deprived of generations of successors has made him very amenable. Seriously though, Helena *mou*, I know he will come to love and value you. So, will you marry me?'

'Oh, yes, Marcos,' she breathed. 'Oh, yes.'

'When?' With one finger he stroked her lips, an incredibly erotic gesture.

'Whenever you like.'

'Just as well,' he commented, with the suspicion of a triumphant smile, 'because you are on your way to your wedding now.'

She ought to have been indignant at his high-handed arrangement of the ceremony, at his assumption that she would meekly go along with his plans, Lena told herself some considerable time later. But she wasn't.

'It was a lovely surprise,' she told Marcos when they were alone once more in the great bed that had seen their first lovemaking, 'and a lovely wedding. But how on earth did you get so many people to be there at such short notice?'

'The moment Domenicos Theodopoulos left my office, I told Lydia to get busy with the arrangements.'

'You were so sure of me?' She could not help the little note of chagrin.

'Should I not have been?' he asked gravely as he took her in his arms.

'No,' she reassured him. Then, 'Oh, I do love you, Marcos.'

He held her tight, cradling her against him, and her instant response ignited the fires of his desire. In a maelstrom of passion they came together, moving in sensual rhythm, his lovemaking wringing cries of ecstasy from her as sensual explosions rocked her, deeper and stronger than before as together they exploded into a tumultuous, simultaneous climax.

Just before she too drifted into sleep, still held within the circle of Marcos's arm, Lena stole a loving look at his relaxed features, the mouth still curved in a smile of peaceful satisfaction. A smile lifted the corners of her own lips as she reflected that the Black Lion of Skiapelos was just a pussy-cat, after all.

Harlequin Presents®

Coming Next Month

1263   A BITTER HOMECOMING Robyn Donald
Alexa returns home to find that Leon Venetos believes all the scandal broadcast about her And he wastes no time showing his contempt in unfair treatment of her Yet Alexa can't fight the attraction that binds them together

1264   WILD PASSAGE Vanessa Grant
Neil Turner, looking for crew for his boat, signs on Serena. He has no idea that although she's lived with sailing for years, it's only been in her dreams. He soon finds out as they start down the west coast of the United States that her practical experience is actually nil!

1265   EQUAL OPPORTUNITIES Penny Jordan
Sheer desperation leads Kate Oakley to employ a man as nanny for nine-month-old Michael, her friend's orphaned baby And while Rick Evans comes with impeccable references, he has his own motives for wanting to be in her life.

1266   WITH NO RESERVATIONS Leigh Michaels
Faced with running the old family hotel, Lacey Clinton soon realizes she isn't properly qualified to restore it. Selling to rival hotelier Damon Kendrick seems the answer—until she learns he doesn't want the hotel unless Lacey comes with it.

1267   DREAMS ON FIRE Kathleen O'Brien
Megan Farrell already dreads locking horns with the new owner of the New Orleans rare book shop where she works. But even she has no idea how easily this man can destroy her firm ideas about the past—and especially those about love and passion.

1268   DANCE TO MY TUNE Lilian Peake
Jan accepts as just another job the assignment of tracking down Rik Steele and reconciling him and his father When she falls in love with her quarry, she has a hard time convincing him that she's not just interested in the money.

1269   LEAP IN THE DARK Kate Walker
When a stranger kidnaps Ginny and the two children she's temporarily looking after, Ginny doesn't know where to turn for comfort. All her instincts tell her to turn to Ross Hamilton—but he's the man holding them captive.

1270   DO YOU REMEMBER BABYLON Anne Weale
Singer Adam Rocqualne, idolized the world over, can have any woman he wants. And it seems he wants Maggie. She knows a brief fling in the public eye would leave her miserable—yet she wonders if she has the strength to say no.

Available in May wherever paperback books are sold, or through Harlequin Reader Service:

In the U.S.
901 Fuhrmann Blvd.
P.O. Box 1397
Buffalo, N.Y. 14240-1397

In Canada
P.O. Box 603
Fort Erie, Ontario
L2A 5X3

Have You Ever Wondered If You Could Write A Harlequin Novel?

Here's great news—Harlequin is offering a series of cassette tapes to help you do just that. Written by Harlequin editors, these tapes give practical advice on how to make your characters—and your story—come alive. There's a tape for each contemporary romance series Harlequin publishes.

Mail order only

All sales final

HARLEQUIN
American Romance®

Live the

Rocky Mountain Magic

Become a part of the magical events at The Stanley Hotel in the Colorado Rockies, and be sure to catch its final act in April 1990 with #337 RETURN TO SUMMER by Emma Merritt.

Three women friends touched by magic find love in a very special way, the way of enchantment. Hayley Austin was gifted with a magic apple that gave her three wishes in BEST WISHES (#329). Nicki Chandler was visited by psychic visions in SIGHT UNSEEN (#333). Now travel into the past with Kate Douglas as she meets her soul mate in RETURN TO SUMMER #337.

ROCKY MOUNTAIN MAGIC—All it takes is an open heart.

THE STANLEY HOTEL— A HISTORY

Upon moving to Colorado, F. O. Stanley fell in love with Estes Park, a town nestled in an alpine mountain bowl at 7,500 feet, the Colorado Rockies towering around it.

With an initial investment of $500,000, Stanley designed and began construction of The Stanley Hotel in 1906. Materials and supplies were transported 22 miles by horse teams on roads constructed solely for this purpose. The grand opening took place in 1909 and guests were transported to The Stanley Hotel in steam-powered, 12-passenger "mountain wagons" that were also designed and built by Stanley.

On May 26, 1977, The Stanley Hotel was entered in the National Register of Historic Places and is still considered by many as one of the significant factors contributing to the growth of Colorado as a tourist destination.

We hope you enjoy visiting The Stanley Hotel in our "Rocky Mountain Magic" series in American Romance.

RMH-1

This April, don't miss Harlequin's new Award of
Excellence title from

elusive as the unicorn

*When Eve Eden discovered that Adam
Gardener, successful art entrepreneur, was
searching for the legendary English artist, The
Unicorn, she nervously shied away. The Unicorn's
true identity hit too close to home....*

*Besides, Eve was rattled by Adam's
mesmerizing presence, especially in the light
of the ridiculous coincidence of their names—
and his determination to take advantage of it!
But Eve was already engaged to marry her
longtime friend, Paul.*

*Yet Eve found herself troubled by the different
choices Adam and Paul presented. If only the
answer to her dilemma didn't keep eluding her....*

HP1258-1